THE
PRINCE
OF
NOWHERE

THE PRINCE OF NOWHERE

ROCHELLE HASSAN

HARPER

An Imprint of HarperCollinsPublishers

The Prince of Nowhere

Copyright © 2022 by Rochelle Hassan

All rights reserved. Printed in Lithuania.

Library of Congress Control Number: 2021949303
ISBN 978-0-06-305460-8

Typography by David DeWitt
22 23 24 25 26   SB   10 9 8 7 6 5 4 3 2 1
❖

First Edition

For Mom—
Thank you for countless trips to the
library, and everything else.

CH. 1

THE CROW HAD CRASH-LANDED UNDER THE CHERRY TREE, his wings half-frozen. Roda found him lying there in the grass while the ice on his feathers melted into a puddle.

He wasn't missing any limbs. No bald spots. His sharp beak and sleek black wing tips were perfectly intact. That meant he couldn't have been lost in the mist for very long.

Anonymous had been right. *Again.*

Roda peeled off her jacket and wrapped the small, cold lump inside, where the material was warm from her body. The crow's eyes were half-open, but he didn't move when she touched him, and that was what made her really worried: he was too hurt to be afraid.

A few feet away, the mist rose into the sky. It formed a

wall that wrapped around the whole town, a perfect circle. But she wasn't used to seeing it up close. She averted her eyes and focused on the crow. The bundle went into her open backpack, which she held on her front. She hopped on her bike and raced home, hunched forward against an icy wind that pricked her face like a thousand needles.

When she glanced over her shoulder, the abandoned mill and the cherry tree were far away, matchbox-sized, but the mist only looked bigger, a swirling white void that swallowed land and sky alike. The fields whipped by in a blur, until the wasteland between mist and town gave way to the first low buildings of Brume. As the mist's biting chill ebbed away, warm air soothed the numbness from her cheeks, nose, and fingers. Her house was a good ten minute ride into town. She'd never have gone anywhere near the mill if not for the letter—the one that had sent her here, to find this crow.

What's so special about you, anyway? she thought, as she glided down a cramped, birch-lined road, passing a dozen cookie-cutter houses until she reached hers. She let her bike fall over in her tiny front yard—long overgrown with dandelions and crabgrass—and peeked into her bag. A mess of black feathers, the dullish gleam of a beak. Still no sign of movement.

In the kitchen, Mom was bent over the paperwork she'd brought home from the office; Aunt Dora balanced a book in one hand and a cup of coffee in the other. They looked up when she burst in.

"Hi," she said breathlessly, placing her bundle on the table near Aunt Dora. The backpack, she dropped into one of the mismatched chairs. She grabbed a bowl from the cabinet, dashed to the sink to fill it with lukewarm water, and ferried it to the table.

"What brings my wayward daughter home so soon?" Mom said. "I've never seen you this excited to get inside the house."

"A life-or-death situation," Roda informed her.

Mom had big brown eyes that gave away all her secrets and a wide smile that felt like home. Her wavy blond hair was swept out of her face, pinned back at the nape of her neck. Roda didn't look a thing like her. She'd gotten her dark curls and blue eyes from Dad, or so she'd heard. She couldn't remember him much, but everyone said Aunt Dora—his sister—looked just like him, and the resemblance between her and Roda was undeniable. Their faces had the same angles, the same slopes, the same pinkish paleness so unlike Mom's tan and freckles. It wasn't uncommon for strangers to mistake Aunt Dora for her older sister.

"Really? What kind of life-or-death situation?" Mom asked, humoring her. "Let me guess. A plague."

"Did you see how she flew in here?" Aunt Dora said. She set down her mug with a light *thunk* and half closed her book, marking her place with her thumb. "*Clearly* being chased by a gryphon."

"No, no, she likes animals too much. She only runs from chores."

Roda kept quiet. They didn't know about Anonymous.

Before they could come up with any more guesses, she gently dug the crow out of the folds of her jacket and placed him into the water to thaw, careful to keep his head above the surface.

Mom put down her pen, frowning.

"Oh," said Aunt Dora. Her eyes went round as coins under the crisp new-paper white of her hair.

Aunt Dora had been about Roda's age when she'd gotten lost in the mist, just like the crow. Her hair had frozen up and its pigment had bled away. Even her eyelashes were white. As Roda examined the crow, using her fingers to comb through his feathers and loosen some of the frost, she found streaks of the same shade of white in his plumage. Those would be permanent, just like it had been permanent for Aunt Dora.

Mom looked at the crow, and then at Aunt Dora, and back again. "Already?"

She spoke so quietly that Roda almost missed it.

"I thought I still had a few days," Aunt Dora said in an undertone. "I lost track of time."

"You, of all people?"

They always talked like that, filling in a conversation that was happening half in their heads. Roda was used to it.

The crow stirred, his wings twitching in the water.

"I'm going to take care of him until he gets better," Roda said. "He can stay in my room."

Mom tapped the edge of the table with a fingernail, again and again, the sounds stringing together like beads on a necklace: *taptaptaptaptap.* "I have it on good authority that crows make terrible houseguests."

"We can't leave him outside to die!"

"He can stay in the living room," Mom said. The tapping ceased. "Right, Dora?"

Aunt Dora flinched, as if she'd forgotten everyone else was there. She'd been studying the crow with a strained, tight-lipped expression. Her brows were drawn together, an unhappy furrow between them.

"While I'm sure he'd prefer more luxurious

accommodations," she said dryly, "the living room will do just fine."

Aunt Dora's fingers tugged absently at a cord around her neck, from which hung a ring, the only piece of jewelry Roda had ever seen her wear. But as soon as Roda's eyes caught the movement, she let go, folding her hands on her lap.

Once the crow was warmed up, Roda dried him off with the softest towel she could dig out of the linen closet, and left him wrapped loosely in a blanket on the windowsill. She thought he'd feel better if he could look outside. He didn't move except to tuck his head under his wing and go back to sleep.

"What are you doing?" Mom asked, as Roda filled a small bowl with water and started cutting up a pear into pieces.

"He needs food," Roda said. "Are you okay?"

"Of course," said Mom. "Why wouldn't I be?"

"You're drinking ginger tea. Fresh," she said, nodding toward the lump of raw ginger resting on a cutting board by the sink. "You only do that when you're stressed."

The smell of honey hung in the air. Mom had both hands wrapped around the biggest mug they owned, and her tan skin had gone pale under the waning sunlight.

"You're too young to be such a worrier," Mom said, with a lopsided smile. "The only thing you should be worrying about is your homework. My sources say you have a quiz tomorrow."

Roda made a disgusted face. "Are you one hundred percent sure your sources are trustworthy?"

"Hmm . . ." Mom tapped a finger against her chin. "Well, my source is the planner I found open on the table last night, which is where you always leave your things, even when I tell you to put them away. Though I suppose it could've belonged to the gremlin that always makes the messes you swear you couldn't possibly be responsible for. It was covered in your handwriting, but maybe the gremlin does forgery on the side?"

"That's probably it." Roda nodded.

"Better study anyway. Just to be safe."

"Fine," Roda said. "I'm only trying to save a life here. But I guess math is more important."

"I'm glad you agree," Mom said. "Get to it."

Fifteen minutes later, Roda was curled up on the couch with her textbook open. Mom sat on the other end with her mug and a stack of paperwork. The sunset had brought rain with it, but she was warm in the living room with the healing crow burrowing into the blanket-lined box she'd made up for him.

Later, Roda would remember every detail of that night: the spicy-sweet smell of ginger, the cushion sagging comfortably underneath her, the way the lamplight drew luminous streaks through Mom's golden hair. A night perfectly preserved in the resin of her mind.

Because, after that, everything changed.

CH. 2

RODA'S NIGHTLY RITUAL INVOLVED SITTING UP WITH A flashlight and reading under the covers until her eyes were so tired that blinking hurt. She'd exhausted most everything of interest in the local library, but Aunt Dora spent a few months of the year traveling—funding her exploits with research grants from universities to track down artifacts linked to long-dead mages—and she always came back with stacks of books. Adventure stories of pirates and knights, histories of ancient civilizations, the occasional poetry collection. They weren't as good as Aunt Dora's stories, but hardly anything was.

Tonight, she left *The Magnificent Tales of Willow the White Wolf* on her desk and huddled in her closet, setting down her flashlight so that it pointed away from the bedroom door. She dragged up the corner of the loose floorboard near the back wall. Underneath was a hollow where she hid her most prized possessions.

These included:

1. A picture of her father, who had died when Roda was barely old enough to walk. There were other photos of him in the house, but this one was just hers.

2. An old-fashioned pocket watch on a chain Aunt Dora had brought her from Uskana that could survive the harshest weather conditions. Not that the weather in Brume was ever anything but mild. She didn't have much use for it, but she liked to think she might need it one day—if she ever found herself crossing the Vipera Sea in the middle of a typhoon or camping on the frozen tundra of Lituun's northern plains, like Aunt Dora had. Unlikely, but a nice thought nonetheless.

3. A bracelet woven for her by a friend a couple of years back. Days later, that same friend had moved away, following her parents onto the train that would take her through the mist, into the beast-ridden lands outside, and then safely past the cloudy border of some other city. She and Roda had traded letters for a few months. Then the letters had tapered off, and they'd lost touch.

Visits were uncommon in the Aerlands. Travel wasn't safe, even with the train guardians around. Even Aunt Dora conducted most of her expeditions outside the Aerlands: places where there was no mist, where it was easier to get around, and where there were more people than monsters. Always, though, crossing their country's border was treacherous. She had to do it on foot because the trains didn't run past the mountains. But she did it anyway, year after year—she was in her early thirties now, but she'd been a teenager when she'd made her first journey abroad. Roda envied her a little. She'd even fantasized about following in Aunt Dora's footsteps, though she knew she'd never be brave enough to do anything of the sort. She'd been nervous just getting *close* to the mist.

Roda pushed aside the bracelet, the photo, and the watch, digging deeper until her fingertips brushed paper. *There.* The latest addition to her hollow under the floor: three notes written in an unfamiliar hand. She unfolded them and smoothed out the creases.

The first one had materialized a few months ago inside her boot, which she'd left on the front porch after a very rainy, muddy walk home. She hadn't realized the scrap of paper was there until she'd shoved her foot inside and her socked toes had brushed against it.

It read:

Dear Roda,

What is a place you can only enter through one door, but can leave through many?

Nowhere.

Nylla will ask you to braid the lavender.
It will rain fourteen minutes after school lets out. Bring a coat.

She'd stared at the careful writing, puzzled. The writer knew her name, but hadn't given their own. And was that supposed to be a riddle?

It was *weird*, but not weird enough to make her late for school. She'd stuffed the note in her pocket, picked up her bike, and gotten to class with just seconds to spare. Year Seven's homeroom had been nearly unrecognizable. Strewn across desks were clusters of violet alliums with their star-shaped blossoms, blue and pink asters with sunny golden centers, yellow buttercups lying with their stems curved like smiles, poppies in red and orange. Her class-mates had pushed their desks into loose groups, chattering as they worked together to weave the flowers into crowns and long, dazzling plaits.

Nylla had waved her over giddily. A stray petal had

caught in her inky black hair, and tiny cuts had littered her brown hands from the roses she was stripping of thorns.

"Who's getting married?" Roda had asked, for these could only be wedding decorations.

"My sister." Nylla had beamed. "This weekend! Will you do the lavender?"

She'd pressed a paper-wrapped bundle of lavender stems into Roda's hands.

"Um, sure," Roda had said, covering her shock as she recalled the letter. Questions crowded her mind, and a touch of nerves.

To distract herself, she'd gotten to work. It was a familiar, soothing task. In Brume, weddings were community events. The couple's immediate family would put in the most work, but everyone pitched in to make the celebration as colorful and lively as they could. Only white and black were off-limits. Black was for death; white was for the mist. When Mr. Worrel had come in and called attendance, he'd accepted a handful of crocuses and let them all go on weaving while he conducted a textbook-free history lesson.

Still, her mind had kept straying to the letter. Since they hadn't signed the note, she started thinking of her correspondent as *Anonymous*. But why write to *her*? She'd spent half the day twisting to look out the window, at the sliver of blue sky visible between the top of the mist and the edge of the window frame. Sunlight funneled down through the vortex, bouncing off the shifting white boundary so it glowed like polished silver. It wasn't going to rain on a day like this. No way.

Five minutes into her ride home, the sky had darkened.

Ten minutes, and thunder had rumbled overhead like an empty stomach.

She'd tilted her head up. Iron clouds rolled above her, lumpy and swollen with moisture.

At fourteen minutes exactly, the clouds broke open and unleashed a torrent of icy rain.

I should've taken the advice about the coat, she'd thought, biking harder and shaking her damp hair out of her eyes. She hadn't known if what she felt was excitement or fear.

As soon as she was inside and dry, she'd fished the note out of her pocket and read it again. It seemed harmless, but she showed it to Aunt Dora anyway. Between her and Mom, Aunt Dora was less likely to panic if something *was* wrong.

But Aunt Dora had said: "Quite the imagination you've got there. Your penmanship could use a bit of work, though."

"It wasn't me!"

Aunt Dora's eyes had crinkled at the corners as she smiled, slyly, like they were both in on a joke. Times like that, Roda didn't think they were anything alike at *all*. She'd snatched the note away with a huff and decided not to mention it again.

A part of her had been relieved, though. She'd done the right thing. She'd told an adult. It wasn't her fault she hadn't been believed. Now she didn't have to feel guilty about keeping the note to herself, and any others that might come along later. It was a secret just for her. This was something of a thrill. In a town where nothing interesting ever happened, even a small mystery felt like a big deal. But she didn't hear from Anonymous again for such a long time that she soon became convinced that it had been a fluke.

The next note had come last month. It was crammed between the spokes of her bike's front wheel, and read:

Dear Roda,

What's a place you must either leave in ten seconds or stay for ten years?

Nowhere.

A family of three followed the train tracks and snuck into Brume today. Your mother will come by the school at lunchtime with the house key, because she's going to be working late.

A new prediction. A new riddle, with the same answer as the old one. And, true to form, Anonymous hadn't bothered with a signature.

She'd wanted to hear from them again, but she wasn't sure she liked this note. Weather forecasts were one thing; bringing up Mom was crossing a line. She shivered, the note crumpling in her hand as her grip tightened. But if Anonymous wanted to hurt her, wouldn't they have done it already?

At lunch, she'd slipped outside and waited on the steps in front of the school building. Mom came up the block minutes later, rolling her bike alongside her as she walked, her satchel over her shoulder and her hair loose. Her eyes were tired, the lines around her mouth pronounced. But she smiled when she saw Roda waiting for her.

"What are you doing out here?" she said, propping the bike against the wall and sinking down next to Roda. "Everything okay?"

"Yeah, I just—I heard about the rail hikers, so I figured—"

"Ah. Word traveled fast today, huh?"

She dug the house key out of her bag and dropped it into Roda's hand.

"I heard it was three of them," Roda said. They propped their bagged lunches on their laps, Roda unwrapping a sandwich and Mom stabbing her fork into her salad.

"Yeah." She speared a piece of carrot and offered it to Roda, who wrinkled her nose but accepted it. "A man and two children."

"Are they okay?"

"I'm not sure. They're in the border clinic being treated right now," she said. "I haven't been allowed to speak with them yet."

If the mist exposure hadn't been too prolonged, they'd get away with bleached hair like Aunt Dora. In the very worst cases, people lost fingers and toes to frostbite or had the blood frozen solid in their veins.

"Where'd they come from?" she asked.

"Vicentia," Mom said, frowning down at her salad like it was the source of all the world's problems. Roda slipped an apple slice into her bowl. Mom blinked, looked up, and grinned. "Don't worry. I'll do what I can for them."

Then she asked Roda about her lessons and her friends. But part of Roda's mind was at Brume's border, where train tracks disappeared into the all-consuming white, trying to imagine who could be desperate enough to cross that boundary and risk disappearing, too.

The Aerlands was a great, broad country of mostly flatlands and lakes that Roda had only ever seen on maps and in pictures. Jagged, impenetrable mountain ranges bracketed the eastern and northern borders, but these, too, were nothing more than strings of tiny black triangles in her atlas. Most of all, it was a land of monsters. Fierce, watchful gryphons that defended their territories to the death. Bloodsucking elephant bats that could sniff out prey from miles away. Golden-hoofed antelopes as tall as trees, and the ghost wolves of the western woods.

The mist was a protective enchantment placed by the legendary mage Aurelion Kader many centuries ago, to defend the human settlements of the Aerlands from those terrors. Each city had a barrier of its own to keep the monsters out. But there were dangers *inside* the mist, too.

Since travel was infrequent and perilous, and the mists jammed electrical transmissions between different cities, the Aerlands was more like a collection of city-states than a unified nation. Each city was mostly self-sustaining, with its own culture and customs. Most of them weren't as peaceful as Brume. Some were riddled with crime, disease, poverty, and corruption; some were dangerously overcrowded, but the mist couldn't expand, so the cities couldn't, either. In Brume, they left a berth between the town and the mist—a buffer consisting of empty fields, some farmland, dovecotes for the carrier pigeons, apiaries. No one liked to live too close to its deadly chill, or look outside and see its creeping tendrils reaching for them. But in Vicentia, the population had grown so much that they used and reused every inch of space available to them. There were buildings erected so close to the mist that the outer walls were permanently coated in frost, and the people who occupied them could feel the cold even in their sleep. Or so Roda had heard.

But you couldn't just pick up and move to another town. Not with all the migratory regulations and the sky-high price of a one-way train ticket.

Mom always said when people braved monsters and mist, it was because they were running from something even scarier. Her job was in the migration control department, and the rules were strict: the number of people allowed into Brume depended on how many of its citizens had died or been born during the previous year. But there was always a little wiggle room, so Mom tried to get as many people to stay as she could. She helped file their residency petitions, placed them in temporary jobs, secured shelter for them while the paperwork went through. If their applications were denied, she usually managed to get the government to pay for their train tickets out. She believed that helping people who fled to Brume for safety was the most important part of her job. Because if you *could* help, then you *should*.

Weeks had passed. Then, yesterday, the third note had appeared. Someone had taped it to the underside of her desk.

It read:

Dear Roda,

What place has an engine that never runs out of fuel and an anchor that can't be cast off?

Nowhere.

After school, go to the abandoned mill on the edge of town. Under the cherry tree out front, you'll find a crow.

He's not dead. Pick him up and bring him home.

Candles at noon.

She'd folded the note and put it away. At noon, when a storm made the power go out, Mr. Worrel produced candles and conducted their literature lesson in the low, flickering light of a dozen flames. Roda hadn't needed any more proof, though. She would've gone looking for that crow either way.

CH. 3

IN THE MORNING, THE CROW WOKE UP.

He didn't like being conscious, and he liked Roda even less. When she stumbled blearily into the living room, half a piece of toast hanging out of her mouth and her jacket dangling off one shoulder, he greeted her with a stream of outraged squawks. She couldn't speak crow, but she guessed those sounds meant something along the lines of: *what is this, where am I,* and most of all, *how dare you?*

She replaced his water bowl and set a fresh plate of fruit and nuts before him. He dove at her hand beak-first; she whipped it away.

"I'm trying to help you!" she said. "You can go if you really want. Go on, then."

She opened the window. He waddled toward the sunny outside world, tail dragging on the windowsill. He fluttered his wings, scraped the blankets with his feet as if preparing to take off—any minute now, he'd fly away—

His wings settled. He turned to his breakfast as if that was what he'd meant to do all along.

"See?" she said. "You can't fly yet. And I'm the one keeping you fed, so be polite."

He made an unpleasant noise, like a croak. She doubted she'd like it much if she knew what it meant, so she decided to interpret it as, *Yes, indeed, kind young lady, I shall be certain to practice my best behavior so long as I remain in your gentle care.*

Her lessons dragged on forever that day. If anyone had asked, she wouldn't have been able to recall a single thing she'd learned. After school, she detoured to the library for a few books on ornithology and returned home with their satisfying weight in her backpack.

She let herself in with the key, which Mom had remembered to give her before work this time. Aunt Dora wasn't home yet. When she was in town, she spent most of her days helping out around the house and doing volunteer work—at the animal shelter, the community gardens, the hospital, or wherever else she was needed. She could be back in five minutes or well past Roda's bedtime.

As Roda replaced the crow's food and water, he watched her warily with one fierce orange eye, so bright it almost looked gold.

"Maybe you're *not* a crow," Roda said, studying him intently. "I've never seen a crow with eyes like that."

The door opened.

"Mom?" she said.

"Just me," Aunt Dora replied, appearing in the doorway. Her white hair was in disarray, her skirts muddy, and her cheeks flushed from the bike ride home. She'd left her boots outside. "How was school?"

"Fine. Were you at the gardens?" Roda asked. "Don't you normally wear overalls for that?"

"Oh, I—forgot them," she said.

"And gloves," Roda added. "You usually borrow one of their spares. But your hands are all—"

Dirt-streaked and, from the stiff way she held them, sore.

"There weren't any spares today, I'm afraid," she said cheerfully.

She went upstairs to change, ruined skirts swishing around her ankles. Roda soon heard a merry whistling from the second floor.

A hoarse voice spoke up from behind her: "She's *weird*."

All her senses went on high alert. Roda spun around—

A boy sat on her windowsill. He wore a costume of some kind, heavy black cloth embroidered with gold and silver like gleaming veins. The blanket nest was squashed under his bottom, and the crow was nowhere to be found.

"Who—" she began, but her questions died in her throat. His eyes were the same unmistakable gold as the crow's.

Footsteps clattered down the stairs. Roda grabbed him by the arm, shushed his squawks of protest, and shoved him behind the couch. For good measure, she took the quilted throw off the back and tossed it over him.

"*Stay there!*" she hissed at his outraged expression, and let the edge of the blanket drop, hiding him from view. She threw herself over the back of the couch, bounced off the cushions, snagged her backpack strap with one flailing hand, and finally rolled upright.

"You want anything special for dinner?" Aunt Dora asked, poking her head around the doorway.

"Nope," Roda squeaked. She yanked a notebook out of her bag and dropped it next to her on the couch. "You decide."

"Something with meat," said a muffled voice. Roda

coughed loudly to cover it up.

"Maybe some soup," Aunt Dora said, lifting one chalk-white brow. "I hope you're not coming down with something."

She vanished into the kitchen. As soon as she was gone, Roda dove behind the couch, knelt down, and ripped the blanket off the boy. He frowned at her.

"She's already seen me," he said.

"She *has*?"

"Yesterday, when you put me by the window."

"As a *crow*!"

"I am *not* a crow," he said, as offended as if she'd called him a cockroach. "I'm—"

"*Shh*. Come with me."

She crept to the doorway, checked that Aunt Dora wasn't coming down the hall, and beckoned for the boy to follow her. At first glance, she'd thought he was covered in soot, but he wasn't. His skin was gray-tinged, a smoky color she'd seen in the flashing depths of storm clouds, but never on a human before. But his sulky expression was human enough. Bluish-black hair flopped over features so sharp they would have drawn blood if you slapped him: a narrow, pointed chin; a slightly too-long nose; prominent cheekbones.

She led him upstairs and into her room, shutting the door as silently as possible.

"Who are you?" she demanded.

"Ignis," he said. He turned a slow circle, eyes darting over the contents of her room. It was nothing special: a bed, a desk, a closet. The pictures tacked on the wall showed the smiling faces of her family and friends, alongside maps Aunt Dora had brought her from all the places she'd been—Uskana, Alterra, Loska Res, and countless others. She loved her room. But the boy's presence, this boy in an outfit that looked like it cost more than her whole house, suddenly made it seem shabby and plain. She flushed, embarrassed.

"Ignis? Is that your name?"

"Obviously," he said, still studying his surroundings and not meeting her eyes.

"Fine. Since you're *obviously* feeling better, maybe you should go," she said, crossing her arms.

He faced her with a small frown.

"Go . . . where?"

"I don't know," she said. "Where were you going before you crashed?"

"Crashed?" His eyebrows drew together. They peaked sharply at the corners, framing his eyes like upside-down check marks. "Oh . . . I was flying, and then I ran into a cloud, and then I was so cold—"

"It wasn't a cloud," she said. "That was the mist."

"The what?"

Her stomach lurched as he looked at her blankly. This was bad. If he'd never been on the inside of the mist before, that meant he'd grown up *outside*. In the wilds of the Aerlands, past the boundaries of the mist-cloaked cities.

But the only things out there were monsters.

"The mist," she explained. "The Aerlands are dangerous. The mist protects us from the monsters out there, but you can't go through it without protection, because you'll freeze up. That's what happened to your hair, by the way."

"My *hair*?" He lunged for the mirror on her closet door and examined himself from every angle, until he found the spikes of white on the side of his head, crossing above his left ear in stripes. "Is it permanent?"

"I'm afraid so."

His face was the picture of horror. "This is a terrible place."

"It's not that bad," she said defensively. "Never mind. Where were you going before you flew into the mist? Where did you come from?"

He went quiet for a long moment, turning away from

the mirror with a thoughtful frown. Then something in him changed. His shoulders hunched, and he looked down, hiding his expression.

"I—I don't know." He seemed to make a conscious effort to unclench his fists. For a second, his fingertips glinted as if with sparks, but then they were gone. She must have imagined it. "I don't remember."

"How can you not remember?"

"I crashed!" he said. "Things are . . . blurry. I just need time to recover." He paced, his shiny boots striking the floor decisively.

"Are you a—a shapeshifter?"

"What? Of course I am." He tilted his head, as if baffled she'd even had to ask. "Where did you find me?"

"By the abandoned mill," she said, without thinking.

He stopped in his tracks. "Why were you there if it's abandoned?"

She hesitated. "A friend told me I should go."

"Why?"

"They knew you'd be there," she admitted.

"Well, who is this friend? Take me to them at once," he commanded.

Roda bristled at his imperious tone. "I can't."

He threw up his hands in frustration. "Why not? They

were expecting me. Maybe I was on my way to see them."

"I doubt it," she mumbled. He glared at her. "Fine! I can't take you to see them because I don't know who they are."

She pulled out the notes. Even as he took them from her, as his fingers traced over the handwriting, she wanted to snatch them back and hide them away. But that wasn't fair. Because what if Anonymous *did* know him? What if all this time, they'd only wanted to use Roda to get to Ignis?

Her heart sank. She'd been so quick to believe she was special somehow, and that was why Anonymous had written to her. Maybe she wasn't special at all, though. Just convenient.

But Aunt Dora would tell her not to assume anything about another person's mind. *Don't put thoughts in their head or words in their mouth*, she'd say.

"Do you recognize the handwriting?" she asked reluctantly.

"No," he said, handing the notes back. "But I need to find out who this person is."

"Good luck," she said, gesturing toward the door.

"I'm not leaving." He folded his arms. "You're my only lead. I'm staying with you until your correspondent shows up again."

"You can't!" she said. "Mom will be furious."

When Mom helped people cross the border, she did it *legally*. She'd never stuffed an outsider into her backpack and smuggled them into Brume.

The enormity of what Roda had done began to sink in.

"If you give me a couple of hours to hunt, I'll bring her an offering and petition for shelter on her territory, the proper way. I brought down a stag once," Ignis bragged. "I'm sure I can win her over."

"No! You have to *promise* not to bring home anything dead!"

"If I promise, then may I stay here?"

She faltered, caught off guard. Her first instinct was to refuse, but she couldn't kick him out when he didn't know where he'd come from or where he was going. Mom *would* be mad if she knew, but Mom was also the one who said you were supposed to help people.

And it was kind of a relief to have someone to talk to about Anonymous who actually believed her.

"Fine," she said. "But you need to be a crow whenever Mom and Aunt Dora are around."

"I'm not a crow."

But she was already at the door, drawing it open inch by careful inch and checking that no one was around. "Come on," she whispered. "We're going downstairs."

His transformation was so quick her eyes couldn't follow it: a liquid-smooth twist of motion, an explosion of feathers, a pulling-*in* like the edges of a cloth being tucked away. Then her unfriendly crow was soaring over her shoulder, nearly clipping her cheek with his wing tip; he glided down the staircase and into the living room.

Roda followed, replaying the conversation in her head and trying to pinpoint the moment when everything had gone completely out of her control.

CH. 4

She didn't see Ignis leave his roost the next morning, but he was waiting for her when she got to school.

"Finally," he said. "That took you forever! Why don't you just fly?"

"What are you *doing* here?" She pulled him aside so he wasn't blocking the doors. Her classmates cast them curious looks as they passed by.

"You said you found one of the notes here. That means your correspondent has been here, too."

"You have to leave," she said. "People are staring."

The bell rang.

"*Leave,*" she said again, but he followed her inside. Pretending not to know him didn't work. He stayed close on her heels, complaining loudly about how sterile and unpleasant "this place" was. The crowd parted for them; her face burned at the whispers they attracted.

She opened the door to Year Seven's classroom. He still wasn't leaving, and everyone had seen them together. She would just have to adapt.

Adapting turned out to consist mostly of lying.

"Mr. Worrel," she said, plastering on a smile as she led Ignis to her teacher's desk. "This is my cousin. He's visiting and doesn't want to miss any lessons while he's away from home. Could he sit in on class with me, please?"

Ignis beamed at him with a sparkling white row of fangs.

"Where did you say he's from?" Mr. Worrel asked, leaning away as far as he could without falling out of his chair.

"West," she said vaguely. Before Mr. Worrel could object, Roda pointed out an empty desk, and Ignis strutted over to it. She made to follow him, but Mr. Worrel flapped a shaky hand at her, beckoning her nearer.

"Ah . . . Is he ill?" he asked under his breath.

"Not at all," she said, feigning surprise. "Why do you ask?"

Mr. Worrel seemed to consider and discard a number of responses that would've likely been rude if Ignis really *were* a normal boy. And Mr. Worrel had no reason to think that he wasn't. *He* had never met a shapeshifter before, either. At last, he settled on, "His eyes are . . . striking."

"Just contact lenses," she said. "It's a fashion statement."

"Oh, I see! Of course, that . . ." He hesitated. "And— perhaps it was a trick of the light, but his teeth, they . . ."

Roda gave him a wide-eyed look of dismay and dropped her voice to an urgent whisper. "Please don't mention that to him. He's very sensitive about it."

Abashed, Mr. Worrel did not press the issue, and she fled to her desk before he could come up with any more questions.

She spent the rest of the day coming up with increasingly wild excuses to explain away Ignis's appearance to her classmates and teachers. She didn't know if they believed her, and not knowing put her on edge. Ignis made her task harder when he broke into the kitchen at lunchtime and dug raw meat out of the freezer. He brought it back to her table and sat down.

"It's *cold*," he said. "And they washed off all the blood! Why would they ruin a perfectly good carcass like that?"

"Is that—" Nylla said, aghast, as Ignis licked sadly at a chunk of pork.

"Haha! Just a joke!" Roda said and dragged Ignis away.

"Where are we going?" His sharp nails cracked through a layer of ice, dug into the meat, and tore off a bite-sized piece, which he tossed in his mouth like popcorn.

"We need to talk. *Alone.*"

"You're very bossy for someone who can't even fly," he told her haughtily, as she shoved him into an empty classroom.

She shut the door with more force than necessary. "If you don't like it here, then go home."

"I told you," he said, deflating. "I can't go home."

A pang of unwanted sympathy made her anger drain away.

"You still don't remember anything?" she asked. "Not at all?"

He shrugged. "Not anything useful. But I can't go back. If I could, I would have already."

"If you want to find whoever wrote those letters," she said, "you have to act normal. Like a human. Or else you'll be chased out of town, and then what will you do?"

"Out of town?" he said. "Why?"

"Because towns are for humans. Mons—" She stopped herself before she could say the word *monster*. She didn't think Ignis was a monster, even though he could shape-shift and ate raw meat. "I mean, everything that's not human is supposed to be outside the mist."

Roda was hiding someone in Brume who wasn't supposed to be here. This was a much bigger secret than Anonymous and the notes; harboring an outsider could have *real* consequences. If anyone else found out what Roda was doing, they might blame Mom, and she could lose her job. The thought made her stomach twist. Roda had never so much as been reprimanded at school, and now she was essentially committing a crime.

But Aunt Dora always said sometimes you had to take risks to do the right thing. And Roda knew helping Ignis was the right thing.

With a sigh, she perched on one of the desks and gestured for him to sit with her. Then she did her best to describe, in excruciating detail, how to pass for human.

"Being a human is hard," he said morosely. "I don't like it."

"No one does."

But he took her warning to heart. Over the next few days, he was on his best behavior as they continued their search for Anonymous. She showed him where she'd found each of the letters. They went back to the cherry tree where he'd crashed. Ignis peered over their classmates' shoulders like a nosy owl every chance he got, studying their handwriting.

But they had no luck tracking down Anonymous, and Roda received no more letters.

The restraint Ignis showed at school was abandoned the moment they set foot at home. She had never met a boy who cared so much about showering. That wouldn't have been a problem, except he kept dipping into Mom's floral shampoo and perfumes.

"If you keep that up, she's going to notice!" Roda warned him one night, having snuck downstairs after Mom and Aunt Dora had gone to bed.

"Everything in this place smells *fake*," Ignis whispered back, reeking of jasmine. "I can't live with the stench of your paints and metals all over me. I simply can't."

When he wasn't stealing Mom's toiletries, he was in his crow form, preening his wings or lining his nest with paper clips, coins, and silverware. Roda kept having to rescue their spoons from him. Once, Roda caught him in Mom's room, pecking at her jewelry box. She scooped him up in her hands, ignoring his affronted squawks, marched downstairs, and practically threw him into his nest.

"What are you *doing*?" she snapped.

His head swiveled around, checking they were alone, before he changed.

"That box was shiny," he told her.

The hardest part was keeping the secret from Mom and Aunt Dora. Especially when Mom cornered her after dinner one night, about a week later. Mom was at the sink, washing the dishes. Aunt Dora had put the kettle on and was collecting three mugs from the cabinet. And Roda had her homework spread out on the table. But her pencil froze over her notes when Mom said, with forced nonchalance: "Are you feeling all right?"

"Um, yeah," Roda said. She bent her head over her work and scribbled something unintelligible.

"Did you get your period?"

"Mom! No!"

"Okay, okay," Mom said. She turned off the faucet and grabbed a dishrag, picking up a glass to dry. "But you've been showering twice a day, sometimes more. You're sure nothing's wrong?"

I hope you're listening, you silly crow, she thought.

After a too-long pause, Roda said, "Showering helps me think."

"Oh. You must have a lot to think about, then."

The glass clinked as Mom returned it to the cabinet. She picked a plate off the drying rack next. The sleeves of her button-up were pushed over her elbows, but one of them had slipped down while she'd done the washing, and the cuff was damp. She hadn't even noticed.

"N-No, it's nothing. I'm fine."

"Right," Mom said, sounding troubled. She turned around, propping her hip against the counter, and still wiping absently at a plate that was probably the driest it had ever been. "I trust you, so I won't pry. But if you were in trouble, you know you could come to me, right? We could talk about it. And I wouldn't be angry. Even if you think you've done something wrong."

"I know," Roda said. "But I'm not in trouble. I promise."

By now, Roda was practically bent double under the weight of her guilt. But Ignis was trusting her with so much. It was his secret as much as hers. Giving it away now would be a betrayal.

Mom turned back to the dishes just as Aunt Dora set Roda's mug down with a soft *tap* that made Roda jump about a foot in the air. Aunt Dora's lips pressed together, as if she wanted to say something. But she didn't.

More than anyone else, Roda wanted to confide in Aunt Dora. She'd know that this lie Roda was telling—it was harmless. Ignis wasn't hurting anyone, and Aunt Dora had done things far more dangerous than hosting a secret houseguest. She was full of stories about trekking through the secret tunnels and ruby mines that laced Uskana's

Razorback Mountains; hiding from bandits in the shallow waters under the wharfs at Aivia, the seaside capital of Loska Res; bartering in the night markets of Kiraquoi.

Plenty of people, including Roda, dreamed of traveling. But hardly anyone ever did it. If you were born in Brume, you didn't grow up to travel the world. You became a farmer, a doctor, or a teacher. And it didn't really matter which one Roda chose, or if she followed in Mom's footsteps and worked for the government. Everyone who lived in Brume led almost identical lives. Aunt Dora was one of the few who got out, because she hadn't been afraid to forge her own path, even if it meant a life of danger and uncertainty. Roda had always admired that about her. Dreaming was very different from actually *doing*.

Every time Aunt Dora left, part of Roda was afraid she wouldn't return. She'd lost her father already. Who said she couldn't lose her aunt, too? But Aunt Dora always came back. Roda could trust her, and she could trust that Aunt Dora would help cover for them now. That she'd understand. Still, something within Roda warned her to keep quiet.

So Roda buried her nose in her homework and didn't say another word.

CH. 5

RODA TRIED TO PAY ATTENTION IN SCHOOL THE NEXT
day, but she was tense and distracted. The whole world
felt off, like a discordant note playing beneath a familiar
tune.

She slumped over her desk, head propped on her hand,
ignoring the conversation between Ignis and one of the
other boys.

"You don't hunt your own food. I don't believe you,"
Darin said, laughing. Ignis had taken to Darin right away
because he had a streak of white in his corkscrew curls,
not unlike the ones Ignis had. Except Darin had gotten
his on purpose in Year Five, after Rasheed had accused
him of being a scaredy-cat for wearing a hat and gloves

on their field trip to the train station on the edge of town. Darin had biked back out to the mist that same day and stuck his head inside.

"It's true," Ignis said. "Mother taught me to skin a deer as soon as I turned five."

"Cool. Maybe you can teach me to hunt, too."

"That's the problem. There's nothing to hunt here."

"There's birds, I guess."

Ignis gasped.

Here we go. Roda winced. But before she could intervene, Mr. Worrel signaled for quiet.

"This is a very important week," he said. "Tomorrow, we're going to have the opportunity to witness something that only happens once every ten years. Does anyone know what that is?"

There was silence as the class racked their brains. What happened once every ten years?

A line of smooth handwriting surfaced in Roda's memory. *What's a place you must either leave in ten seconds or stay for ten years?*

Goose bumps pebbled over her arms. Could Mr. Worrel be Anonymous? Mr. Worrel, with his infinite repertoire of puns and three cats whose pictures were prominently displayed on his desk, and who never made it through a lesson without dropping or spilling something? Other than the tuft of white hair above his widow's peak, which suggested he'd been daring enough to approach the mist at least once in his life . . . he was the least mysterious person in the world, and he couldn't have anything to do with Roda's letters. She was just being paranoid. Ignis was getting into her head, that was all.

Darin thrust his hand into the air. "Kader's Comet."

"Correct!" Mr. Worrel said. "Starting tomorrow, Kader's Comet will cross the sky once every night, for three nights in a row, and then it'll be gone for another ten years. This is one of the few celestial bodies that can be seen from Brume with the naked eye."

He instructed them to open their textbooks to page 503 and launched into his lecture.

"If the name *Kader* sounds familiar to you, it's for good reason," he said. "Aurelion Kader, the renowned mage who enchanted the mist, was also an accomplished astronomer whose discoveries . . ."

Roda stared down at diagrams of the night sky, lost in thought. She'd only ever seen stars in pictures. The mist soaked up the town's light pollution, magnifying it, and funneled it up like a torch. Brume's night sky was always a flat navy blue, or leaden with clouds that sometimes hung so low they sat atop the mist like a lid on a paper cup. And no one went outside the mist for something as trivial as stargazing. Unless you were Aunt Dora, who didn't think anything was trivial, least of all the stars.

Roda tore her eyes away from the map of constellations she'd never see. Mr. Worrel strode through the rows and passed out permission slips.

"I've spoken with Schoolmistress Bannister," he said. "She's given me permission to keep Year Seven late tomorrow. We'll head to the observatory for an astronomy lesson and then come back here to the school, where we'll watch Kader's Comet make its decennial voyage. It's not a required activity, though I hope those of you who go home take a peek out your windows tomorrow night. It's worth staying up for, I promise."

Ignis accepted his permission slip with an expression of vague distrust, his pointy eyebrows scrunched together, like he'd never seen one before. He probably hadn't. Mr. Worrel smiled—Ignis had grown on him—and moved on.

Ignis's head swiveled around so he could point his startling golden eyes at her. "We're going to watch, right?"

"You want to?"

"Yes," he said firmly. He treated all his opinions like declarations. It made Roda a little envious. Ignis never shied away from saying what was on his mind, and he didn't care what anyone else thought. "I want to spend a night doing something other than spying on your neighbors from your window."

She shrugged. "Sure. I don't think Mom will mind if I stay. After she signs my form, I can just trace the signature onto yours, too."

Now that she was a practiced liar, why not throw a little forgery into the mix?

The next morning, Mom sat at the table, propping her head up with her arm and prodding listlessly at the plate of eggs Aunt Dora had slid in front of her. Her coffee mug was empty, but it hadn't woken her up any, it seemed. Aunt Dora left her own meal untouched in favor of tugging distractedly at the cord around her neck. The ring was tucked into her collar, but Roda didn't have to see it to know it was there. She'd only ever caught glimpses of it over the years, but she could picture it clearly in her mind's eye: plain, durable metal crowned with a blue stone. She'd asked once where it had come from. It had been the one and only time that Aunt Dora had refused to tell her a story.

"Eat," Aunt Dora told Mom. "You look like you need the energy."

"Are you going to work today?" Roda asked, scarfing down her own breakfast.

"I'm going to try," Mom said. She rubbed at her eyes. "Maybe not."

"Okay. I'll be home late tonight. Can you sign this?"

"What? Why?" She squinted at the permission slip Roda had placed in front of her, as if she'd forgotten how to read.

"There's a comet tonight and we're staying in class late to watch." As an afterthought, she added, "Can I?"

Mom had never objected to field trips or after-school activities before. But something about the permission slip made Mom drop her fork with a clatter. She lifted her head out of her hand, eyes wide and completely awake.

"That's tonight?" She turned to Aunt Dora. "Why didn't you tell me?"

Aunt Dora laid a hand over Mom's. "I didn't want—"

She cut herself off abruptly and pressed her lips together. Mom's expression was oddly fragile, like she was on the verge of tears. Roda had never seen Mom cry before. Not even when she talked about Dad.

"It's going to be all right," Aunt Dora said at last, giving her hand a squeeze.

"You should have said something," Mom said. Her voice shook.

Aunt Dora gave her a meaningful look, the kind that said, *we'll talk about this later.* Then she drew out the pen she kept tucked into the side of her boot, pulled Roda's permission slip closer, and signed it herself in her illegible lilting script.

"Do you know what time you'll be able to see the comet?" she asked Roda.

"I think at ten?"

"That's right. Kader's Comet passes over us at ten o'clock tonight," Aunt Dora said, slowly and clearly, "and eleven the next night, and at midnight the next. There is a ten-second window before it crosses the sky and disappears again."

"Um, Okay," Roda said, getting up to rinse her plate.

"Aren't you going to tell her?" Mom burst out.

"Well—"

Roda's plate clinked against the bottom of the sink. "Tell me what?"

"Nothing," Aunt Dora said. She folded the signed permission slip into the front pocket of Roda's backpack. "You're going to be late."

"But—"

"We can talk about it tonight."

"Fine," Roda muttered. She turned on the tap. If it could

wait until later, then it couldn't be *that* important. "Mom, maybe you should go to the doctor. You don't look like you're feeling well."

"I'm fine," Mom said, with a heavy sigh. She pushed her plate away.

"You can go tomorrow if you're not better by then," Aunt Dora said. "Let's not worry about it right now. Have a good day at school."

Roda slung her backpack over her shoulder and headed for the doorway. There, she stopped for a moment and looked back. Mom glared at Aunt Dora through red-rimmed eyes. Aunt Dora only smiled sadly in response. The morning light through the window framed the two of them, one golden-haired and one white, one slumped in defeat and one holding her head high, a symmetry so perfect it belonged in a painting.

She had a bad feeling in her chest, all tight and fluttery. Something in her said: *don't go.*

Then Ignis squawked impatiently from the living room. She was out of time.

Tonight, she told herself as she left. Tonight, she'd insist on the truth, and she'd find out what was going on.

CH. 6

IT WAS A SPUN-GLASS NIGHT MADE OF BLUES AND DARK greens and gray violets. Mr. Worrel led them out onto the field behind the school building. He signaled for them to stop in a spot near the middle of the field, away from the streetlights but still within sight of the school's windows.

"You can spread out, but stay close enough to hear me," he said. There was a shuffle as they obeyed, laying out blankets and opening packets of candy and chips to share. Roda dropped her backpack on a strip of grass near the outer edge of the group.

Ignis sat next to her, even though he'd gone most of the day without saying a word.

"Are you all right?" she asked under her breath.

He shrugged. "It's been over two weeks since I got here."

"Oh." She hadn't realized it had been that long. "So?"

"So, there still haven't been any more letters, and we don't have any idea who Anonymous is! Doesn't that bother you?"

His eyes blazed like fire. She didn't have a chance to respond before Mr. Worrel signaled for them to quiet down.

"We only have a few minutes before Kader's Comet will appear," he said. "In the meantime, open your books to page—"

Roda tuned out the discussion. She folded up her blanket, put it on her backpack, and used it as a pillow. After a moment, Ignis lay back, too. The other students blocked them from Mr. Worrel's view.

The top of the mist was a swirling rim around a bowl of flawless night sky. She folded her hands on her stomach and inhaled the scent of the field, fresh-cut grass and clean air.

The sounds of Mr. Worrel firing off questions and her classmates calling out answers faded to background noise. She could almost filter them out and focus on the voice of the night: the chill breeze rustling their clothes, the chorus of the toads in the pond past the fence, the *whir* of a cricket.

"Maybe Anonymous is gone," she said.

"They *can't* be gone."

"Why not?"

He didn't respond.

"You're being weird today, and I don't think it's just about the letters," she said. "You don't have to tell me what's really wrong. But you can if you want to."

She watched him out of the corner of her eye, not daring to turn her head. He fidgeted, and was quiet for so long she was almost sure he wouldn't reply, until:

"What I told you before," he said, haltingly, "about my—"

But he was interrupted by the exclamations of the other students as Kader's Comet appeared.

It was bright white with a faint tail, scurrying over the sky like a beetle. It arced over their heads and then plummeted past the border of the mist, out of sight once again.

That's it? she thought. It was a lot of hype for something that only lasted a few seconds.

She gathered up her things and walked back across the field with Ignis and her classmates. Exhaustion weighed down her muscles and made her slow, like she was wading through syrup. She rubbed at her eyes.

"What were you saying before?" Roda asked.

"Never mind. It was nothing," he said brusquely.

"It's just, there's no way of knowing if I'll ever get another letter," she said. They fell behind the rest, trudging slowly along in the dark. "Maybe we should focus on helping you remember whatever you forgot. If you really think whoever's writing to me might be someone you know—"

"Just drop it."

"Do you want to figure this out or not?"

"Maybe I don't!"

"Then what are you still doing here?" she asked, more harshly than she'd intended. She tried to soften her next words. "You act like you hate it here, and sometimes you seem so . . . sad."

"If you want me to leave, you should just say so."

"I don't," she said weakly. The truth was, she didn't know whether she wanted him gone or not. Ignis had disrupted her life in so many ways. Sometimes he was downright embarrassing to be around in public. And sometimes he was easier to talk to than almost anyone she'd ever met. She never felt awkward or out of place around him.

But right now, his expression reminded her of a storm—cloudy, obscure, and dark.

"Very convincing," he said. "You're right. I don't know what I'm doing here, wasting time at your pathetic school and living in that shack you call a home—"

"I don't know what's wrong with you, but don't take it out on me!"

"Nothing's wrong!" he snarled.

"So you're acting like this for no reason? Good to know." She sped up, leaving him behind. "You're right. I *don't* want you here. You're obnoxious, rude, self-centered—"

A *whoosh* of air made her turn around just in time to see a small, dark shape take flight. Ignis had left.

Like a lightning strike, the anger was gone as quick as it had come. She biked home alone, wondering—as she often did when it came to Ignis—how things had spun out of her control so fast.

Ignis would come back, she told herself. They'd talk, once they'd both cooled down, and work things out.

Brume at night was soothing as a dream. The glow of the streetlights intensified the dark and pulsed on the fringes of her vision as she passed by. Cold wind snaked under her jacket, making her shiver. She wheeled around the corner and onto her block, where the twin birch rows stood still and watchful as sentries. They caught the light of the streetlamps on their crowns, creating a tunnel of darkness beneath the arch of their branches. She got home, unlatched her gate, and rolled her bike up the path between the weeds.

The windows were dark. Not a single sound disturbed the night. Her eyes scanned her house for any sign of life or movement within and found none.

Something was wrong.

Each step up the path took a monumental effort; her feet wanted to run in the opposite direction. She pushed open the unlocked door, dropped her bag inside, and switched on the hall light. The house was eerily quiet: after-a-thunderstorm quiet, quiet like it had been abandoned. Even the pipes in the walls and the creaky floorboards had nothing to say.

Mom wasn't in the living room, and neither was Ignis, his nest in the windowsill lying empty. Her footsteps on the stairs were deafeningly loud in the silence, and it made her nervous, as if someone unseen might hear her and know she was alone.

She checked the bedrooms—deserted. Her clammy fingers slipped on the handle as she threw Mom's door open last. Empty. Mom's work bag was missing from the dresser, so she must have left this morning. But she'd never come back. Fear thrummed through Roda's body, burning away all traces of drowsiness.

She trudged down the stairs again, numb, her hand dragging down the banister. Maybe she was overreacting. But Aunt Dora had said they'd talk tonight, and Mom wouldn't have let Roda come home this late to an empty house. Not without borrowing one of her office's carrier pigeons to send word to her at school.

She flicked on the kitchen light. There was a shape slumped over the table—a person—

Mom.

It was as if she hadn't moved since Roda had seen her that morning. She sat in her work clothes, her hand curled around her coffee mug.

Roda was across the room in a flash, leaning over Mom's limp form, pulling at her shoulders so she could sit her up and look at her face. Her head lolled; her eyelids didn't so much as flutter. She bent close to listen to her breathing. It was there, but faint and slow. Her hair flopped over her face, and her thin lips were parted slightly. The lines around her mouth and eyes seemed deeper, as if, in sleep, she'd aged.

Nothing could have prepared Roda for this. All those times she'd been afraid of losing Aunt Dora the way she'd lost her dad, it had never once occurred to her to worry about Mom. Her mother was the dependable one, the predictable one—their anchor.

Invisible hands wrung out her heart like a rag. Mom wasn't waking up, and Aunt Dora was nowhere to be found. There was no way around it. She had to go get help.

Then she saw the note.

She reached for it and stopped. Her hand hovered, trembling, over the tabletop. A few lines of familiar, tidy handwriting marched across the page. It was from Anonymous. Anonymous had been here, inside her house—in the same room as her mother.

She picked up the note and read it. Then she blinked, tears slipping down her face almost without her noticing them. She read it again, but no matter how hard she tried, the words made no sense at all.

Dear Roda,

What can put a person to sleep forever?

A very rare poison.

If you want her to wake up:
Return to the place where you rescued Ignis.

Dig under the roots of the cherry tree; find what I buried there.
It's yours. Take it, and climb to the top of the mist.

When Kader's Comet crosses the sky tomorrow night, catch it.
You'll only have one chance, so don't be late.

Open the door. I'll be waiting for you.

CH. 7

SHE GRABBED HER POCKET WATCH, A FLASHLIGHT, THE
other letters, and her backpack stuffed with enough food
and water to last a day or two. Then she locked the front
door and set off on her bike.

Shadows played tricks on her eyes, which still stung
with tears. The silence was dense but not absolute, and
every rustle or snap sent ripples of fear through her.

She clutched the handlebars tighter, pedaled harder.
Her bike carried her past Brume's outskirts and onto the
narrow dirt road that led to the mist. A sea of long grasses
swayed on either side. Only the faint glow of moonlight
through the mist alleviated the dark, but even so the night
pressed down on her; being in an open space made her feel

somehow more trapped, not less. She held her flashlight between her palm and the handlebars and chased the end of its beam.

By the time she reached the cherry tree, the tears had dried and her muscles were burning. Roda jumped off her bike and let it fall against the tree trunk. Anonymous had been gracious enough to leave a spade there, in the same hollow spot between the roots where she'd once found Ignis crumpled and half-dead. She dug into the soft soil. Her arms tired quickly, but she only had to break through the first couple of inches before the blade struck something solid. A box.

Freeing it took some maneuvering. In her haste, Roda dug her fingers into the dirt around its edges, trying to loosen it, before she gave up and kept working away with the spade. Her hands shook. All she could think about was how much time she was wasting.

Couldn't you have found a better way to get this to me? she thought, blinking back angry tears.

When she finally pulled the box free and tore open the lid, she found a stack of carefully folded clothing. Boots. Insulated pants. A long-sleeved thermal shirt. A heavy down coat, with elastic wrists and fastenings around the neck. Gloves. A fur-lined hood. A wrap for her face, and goggles to protect her eyes. That was the trick to getting through the mist: covering up every inch of exposed skin and staying warm.

Seeing the clothes made it all feel so much more real. This wasn't a nightmare. She wasn't going to wake up. If she wanted Mom back, she really had to do this.

What if they're lying? Roda thought. *What if I do what they tell me and I still don't get Mom back?*

But Anonymous had never lied to her. It was Roda's own fault she'd mistaken honesty for good intentions.

Aunt Dora wouldn't run away from this, she reminded herself. Aunt Dora wouldn't be afraid. She'd do whatever it took to save Mom. In fact, that was probably why she hadn't been at home. Maybe she'd gone after Anonymous herself. Maybe Roda would find her in the mist, and they'd save Mom together.

Trying not to think too hard about what she was doing and what would come next, she dressed. As she fastened the coat, a piercing call startled her. A black blur whipped past her face, so close the wind made her hair flutter. In midair, the crow transformed into Ignis, who alighted on his feet with surprising grace.

"What are you *doing?*" he demanded.

"I don't see how that's any of your business."

She was still angry about the things he'd said earlier. And where had he been when she'd been panicking in her deserted house next to her unconscious mother?

"Why are you out here so late?" he persisted, pointy eyebrows pulled together in a scowl. "And where did you get those clothes? It's not cold enough to be dressed like that."

"Maybe you'd know what was going on if you hadn't thrown a tantrum and stormed off earlier!"

Her eyes burned. She focused on tying the laces on her boots. They fit perfectly—everything did—as if Anonymous had somehow gotten hold of her exact measurements.

Ignis cocked his head sideways in a very birdlike gesture and studied her.

"What happened?"

She dug the note out of her pocket and thrust it at him. He read it.

A smile spread over his face, revealing his fangs. "This is perfect."

"How can you say that?"

"This is what we wanted!" he said. "We're finally going to find out who wrote these letters."

That's what you *wanted*, she almost said. *I never wanted this. I never wanted to know who they were. I didn't even want to write them back.*

"It's nonsense," she said. "Or worse—a *riddle*. Climb the mist? Catch the comet? Anonymous is playing games with my mom's life."

"We can *win* a game," Ignis said, undaunted. "What are you waiting for? Let's go!"

"You're coming?"

"This is the second time they've written about me," he said, brandishing the note. "I'm part of this, too."

Maybe she would've argued if they'd had time for that. Instead, she said, "Fine. Lead the way."

Past the cherry tree, the road curved like a lock of hair, the end vanishing into white nothingness. The mist towered over them, an opaque wall of cloud. Even though the mist barrier was fixed, never coming any nearer to Brume, it felt alive—its tendrils swirled together, stroked at the ground, made abstract shapes that dissolved almost as soon as they formed. There was so *much* of it. It filled her whole field of vision. She had to crane her neck all the way back to see the sky.

She had delayed putting on the scarf, hood, and goggles, but now she donned them. The scarf wrapped around the lower half of her face and tucked into the high neck of her coat. The goggles suctioned to her skin, creating an airtight seal around her eyes. Finally, she snapped the hood onto the neck of the coat and pulled it up over her face. There was a cord to tighten it, so that it wrapped snug over her forehead. She held the flashlight in one hand, her bag over her shoulder, her pocket watch around her neck.

"Ready?" Ignis said. She started to answer him and then paused, dismayed.

"Wait. You can't go into the mist dressed like that."

Anonymous had only left clothing for Roda. Ignis had no protection.

He turned to her with a startled frown.

"You still don't know what I am?"

"A shapeshifter, like you said."

"Yes, but I'm not *only*—just come on," he said. "I'll show you once we're inside."

And without making any attempt to cover his face or hands, Ignis plunged into the mist.

CH. 8

SHE WOULD'VE BEEN LESS ALARMED IF HE'D BURST INTO flames. Forgetting to be afraid, she broke into a run, following him through the diffuse outer layer and into absolute oblivion.

She couldn't see more than a few feet around her in any direction. Ignis was a shadow behind a veil of mist. Her flashlight washed his silhouette in gold, but only when the currents shifted could she make out his features again. His black hair was still black, his skin untouched by frost. He was as comfortable here as he had been out in the open.

"How are you doing that?" she asked, voice muffled through the scarf.

He eyed her suspiciously. "Promise you won't panic."

"I'm too tired to panic."

After everything that had happened, she felt wrung out, unable to summon any emotion stronger than mild curiosity. A beat passed while they watched each other—Ignis bare-faced with shoulders hunched defensively, Roda bundled up and stiff as a mannequin, wishing she could at least take the goggles off.

Then he closed his eyes. The tendrils of mist brushing playfully against him melted away, until he seemed to be inside a bubble—an invisible barrier that kept the mist at bay. Webs of light crackled over his skin, delicate as spider silk, and then coils of it that snapped and bit like snakes, streaking up through his hair and winding down his limbs—

It was lightning.

When he opened his eyes, they glowed.

"Well?" he said, cranky and impatient as ever. "Say something."

Now she was glad her face was covered; she didn't want him to see her dumbstruck expression, or how huge her eyes had gone behind her goggles. "You're an Aethon."

Aethons were legendary avian beings with lightning powers. They mostly kept to the mountains; beyond that, not much was known about them, except that they were dangerous, like everything else that existed outside the mist. She hadn't ever heard that they could take on a human form. Or that, as birds, they'd be the size of crows, small enough to nest on her windowsill. Maybe if she'd known that, she would have recognized Ignis for what he was sooner.

"I can use my powers to stop the mist from affecting me," he said. "Last time, I'd been flying for days. By the time I got here, I was too tired and confused to protect myself. That's when I crashed."

"Then what are you still doing here?" she asked. "Why don't you just fly to the top of the mist?"

"*You're* the one with the letters," he said. "You're the only one Anonymous talks to. If I want to find them, I have to stick with you."

"Let me see the note again," she said. "Maybe there's a clue about what we're supposed to do next."

He passed it over, but it didn't make any more sense now than it had when she'd found it. With a sigh, she folded it up and stuck it in her pocket.

The mist swirled counterclockwise around Brume, and so that was the direction Roda and Ignis went, too. Even as her flashlight seared a golden path through the fog, the shifting currents made ominous shapes around the outer edges of its beam. She wished she could turn it off. It was too bright and harsh in the soft, moving darkness, and she was worried they'd be seen by the guards that patrolled Brume's perimeter for rail hikers.

After an hour of walking, it became apparent that there was nothing climbable about the mist. Nothing solid or substantial. No hidden staircases or magical portals.

And no trace of Aunt Dora.

Roda stopped, unable to take even one more step forward.

"What?" Ignis asked. Lightning played across his face and over his knuckles like yellow-white veins.

"I bet whoever wrote those letters is laughing at us right now," she said, suddenly furious. "It's mist. You can't climb it. They're messing with us."

She picked at the scarf, feeling suffocated. And the goggles blocked the sides of her vision, so she had to turn all the way left or right if she wanted to see anything other than straight ahead.

"Maybe I could fly us both up," Ignis said.

"Could you carry me?" Roda asked, incredulous.

"I'm not sure. I've never tried it before."

She pictured herself dangling from Ignis's talons by the hem of her sleeve, his small wings flapping wildly.

"Let's not risk it," she said. "Are we missing something obvious? Is *climb* a metaphor?"

She pointed her flashlight up. The mist swallowed the beam just a few feet over their heads.

"This is useless." Ignis cupped his hands around his mouth and shouted: "HELP US!"

"Stop that!" she hissed. "Do you want to get us caught?"

"Who cares? At least then something would be *happening*."

"That's a lot of confidence for someone who fell out of the sky and lost all his memories last time you were here!"

"I didn't—" He bit back whatever he'd meant to say next.

"What?" she said. "What didn't you do?"

"Nothing!"

"You were going to say something earlier. At school."

"I told you, it's nothing." At his side, his fingers curled and uncurled anxiously, throwing off sparks. "It's not important."

"You keep hiding things!" she said. "You—and Aunt Dora, and whoever wrote these notes—I'm sick of people keeping secrets from me!"

"Now who's going to get us caught?"

"Stop changing the subject!"

"You're so bossy! Do you ever shut up?"

She shoved him. Electricity bit her palms even through the gloves; she gasped and jerked back.

Ignis looked deeply offended. "What is *wrong* with you?"

"Oh, I don't know!" she said, throwing her hands up. "What could have possibly happened recently that might have upset me?"

"If you're so worried about saving your mom, maybe you shouldn't push away your only friend!" he said. "*Literally.*"

"How do I know you're my friend when you won't tell me anything?" she said. "Maybe *you* did this. Maybe you wrote those letters and all of this has been some big joke."

Ignis laughed harshly. "You've lost your mind."

"So then tell me the truth! Tell me what you're hiding!"

"I don't have to tell you anything," he said. The fog drifting over his face failed to dampen the effect of his burning gold eyes.

"Then get away from me!" she said. "I can't trust you."

"Is that what you really want?" Ignis asked. His voice had gone cold; even the crackle of lightning over his skin had a frosty quality, like dead twigs snapping underfoot in wintertime.

"*Yes*," she said, and knew instantly that she didn't mean it.

But it was too late to take it back. Ignis stormed away and was gone before she could find the words to stop him.

It doesn't matter, Roda told herself in the ringing silence he left in his wake. She pretended she couldn't feel the way her eyes burned. *Always running away. Who needs him?*

But she had been kind of mean to him, which bothered her, because Roda didn't make a habit of being mean to people. Ignis just brought the *worst* out of her.

As the seconds ticked past, the last of her anger was swept away by a wave of regret. She knew she had to keep going, but she didn't move. Part of her was convinced he'd come back. Any minute now. He had last time, hadn't he?

But this time *wasn't* like their fight before. This one had been her fault.

Her feet started carrying her forward before she made the conscious decision to go after him. But that was what she had to do. Ignis had been the one to come after her before; now, it was her turn. *She* had to be the one to find him.

"Ignis!" she called. But Ignis had chosen now, of all times, to be quiet.

Her search led her much deeper into the mist than she'd

dared go before. The mist thinned until it was as insubstantial as steam. Its delicate outermost layers still hid the world beyond Brume from her view, but only just. If she ventured much farther—far enough to see the outside—she'd catch her first glimpse of the moonlit wilderness crisscrossed by train tracks, maybe even the distant shapes of neighboring towns, concealed behind their own misty barriers.

"Please tell me you didn't go out there," Roda said under her breath.

A little farther on, a dark shape became visible through the fog: a house. Her flashlight's glow bounced off something reflective—a window, and then, lower, a pond. Roda traced its bank with her light, and then pointed it out at the other side.

The mist ended a few feet over the water. Her light pierced through it, beaming out over the pond's inky dark surface. Heart thudding against her ribs, Roda turned away, aiming her flashlight back toward the front door of the abandoned cabin.

It is *abandoned, right?* she thought uneasily.

Its windows were caked with a layer of grime so thick she couldn't even see through the panes. The roof looked on the verge of caving in.

"Ignis?" she called.

No answer.

If Ignis had found this place, then he would've gone inside. She couldn't leave without checking.

Dread paralyzed her. Every instinct told her to turn back, but worse than the thought of going inside that cabin was the idea of wandering around, lost and aimless and alone, while Mom's time ran out.

Aunt Dora wouldn't have hesitated. She wouldn't have let them split up in the first place.

Roda took a deep, steadying breath, and then she jogged up the creaky steps to the covered porch.

The front door was crooked and loose on its hinges, as though someone long ago had forced their way in. The mist swirled through the inside of the house. Two steps into the hall, she sneezed violently. The place was coated in a thick layer of dust and choked with the musty smell of rot.

She pointed her flashlight at the ground, searching for footprints in the dirt.

And she found some. But they didn't belong to Ignis.

These were massive, misshapen prints, each different from the last, as if a parade of creatures had come marching through this hall. None of them were remotely the size or shape of a human's. Or an Aethon's.

Cold sweat broke out on the back of Roda's neck. The hand holding the flashlight trembled.

"Ignis?" she said, but her voice was weak.

What would Aunt Dora do?

She ventured deeper into the cabin, but she didn't try calling Ignis's name again. Disturbing the silence seemed like a terrible idea. The flashlight carved a path for her as she waded through the mist, passing a small kitchen with a wide basin for a sink and a window crusted with dirt. Beyond that was a room that had been stripped of all furnishings, so she had no idea what it might have been before, but now it was filled to bursting with piles of old coins, all gleaming copper, bronze, silver, and gold; jewelry, from simple bracelets to decadent diamond-studded necklaces; picture frames with the photos torn out; metal wires; mirrors of every shape and size; shards of colored glass.

Someone had done this deliberately. Someone *lived* here, in this dusty broken house within the freezing mist. It should have been impossible.

Her gaze fell on an open door. Swallowing hard, she crossed the room and stood at the threshold. A staircase led down into pitch blackness.

Then a flash of bright white light threw the bottom of the stairs into sharp relief, blinding and sudden and accompanied by a *boom*.

"Get away from me!" Ignis bellowed. She couldn't see him from where she was. The flash of light came again, stronger, with a *boom* so loud it made the floor shake under her feet.

Something was down there with him. Something his lightning powers couldn't stop.

CH. 9

SHE FLEW DOWN THE STAIRS, HER BOOTS POUNDING ON the rickety steps and her gloved hand sweeping dust off the railing. Her flashlight's beam cut the dark in half and illuminated the far corner of the basement.

Ignis huddled there, his back to the wall, black hair damp with sweat. Something stood between him and the stairs, blocking his only exit.

The hulking figure that advanced on Ignis shifted and changed so rapidly it was hard to process what she was seeing. Its body was a roiling mass of fur, then scales, then shiny rubberlike skin, then tough, leathery hide. It was broad and muscular, and then it was slender and sinuous. It had four legs, then six, then two, then four again.

A gasp must have escaped her, or maybe a whimper, because it spun away from Ignis—and turned on her instead.

It had a hundred faces, each fighting for the prime position at the front of the creature's head. Each face gazed at her for a split second—a snout, and then fangs; a lush mane of golden-brown fur, and then snakelike eyes, slanted and piercing—before it sank away into the shapeshifting body, to be replaced by another. The faces never disappeared completely, but slid aside to make room for the next, covering the monster's neck and torso and upper back with rolling eyes and gaping, fanged mouths.

For an instant, she caught sight of a face that was almost human, ash-skinned and golden-eyed.

Roda screamed. The flashlight fell from her numb fingers, clattered on the floor, and rolled up to the creature's feet.

The monster did not like that. It roared with a hundred voices and lumbered toward her, surprisingly fast, even though its feet changed beneath it with every step it took. It ate up the distance between them. Roda scrambled back up the stairs, but then it was right there, leaping over the first three steps in one go.

The heel of her boot caught against the next step, and she fell.

Her gloved hands groped for leverage, slipped, and she looked down into a hundred pairs of eyes, a hundred starving open mouths inches from her kicking feet—

The monster howled and faltered. Ignis had leapt on its back, grasped a fistful of fur, and bashed one of its faces with the flashlight. Something broke with a sickening *crack*, maybe a nose or a jaw. Blood dripped onto the stairs.

"What are you doing? *RUN!*" Ignis yelled. He beat at it with the flashlight again and again. It tried to buck him off, but its paws turned into talons, and it slid down the stairs. Ignis climbed over it, clutching the bloody flashlight.

Roda snapped out of it, dashing up the stairs with Ignis at her side.

And then—

A clawed hand grabbed her ankle.

It dragged her to the ground again. The breath was knocked out of her as she landed on her belly, pain lancing up her arm from where her elbow hit the ground. She shrieked, kicking, but it was no use. The creature's grip was tight.

It tugged. She slid down two steps.

Ignis was almost at the door, but he stopped at the

sound of her screams. He doubled back and grabbed her outstretched hand.

Their eyes met for the briefest moment. Then he pulled, nearly hard enough to yank her arm out of its socket. She kicked again and this time her foot connected with something soft. The monster howled with all its voices. Its grip loosened and she shot to her feet.

Ignis pulled her up the stairs. Downstairs in the dark, the monster moved, regaining its balance. She and Ignis slammed the door shut.

"Get something to hold this," he said, breathless, putting his weight against the door. "I'll stay here and make sure it doesn't get through."

"Okay," she wheezed, running to the piles of shiny metallic things that had to be the monster's hoard. She picked up the end of an empty chest and dragged it to the basement door. Then she brought things to fill it: a heavy lamp, as many coins as she could carry in a silvery cape she found draped over a stool, an assortment of ornate goblets and flagons that had been heaped carelessly into a corner.

The monster pounded at the door, which shook and groaned. Ignis leaned against it still, teeth gritted and sweat dripping down his face. The chest was heavy, but not heavy enough; Ignis was the only thing keeping the door shut.

"This isn't working," he said. "I'm going to try something else."

He plucked one of the silver coins from the chest and pressed it against the edge of the door where it met the frame. His hand glowed white, and when he pulled away, the coin had melted in place. Panting, he did it again. That one took him longer to melt, and he had to lean against the door after.

"Ignis, that's enough," she said uneasily. "Let's go. You've slowed it down. We can get away if we run."

"It's *fast*," he told her. "And the mist doesn't bother it. We need to make sure it can't get out for a long time, or we won't be able to lose it."

Roda took over holding the door. He kept working on the coins, welding them against the seam of the doorframe, until it was dotted up and down with molten silver and gold. He fused more coins into the hinges for good measure. The banging continued, but the door didn't budge.

Satisfied, Ignis sank to the ground. He leaned against the wall.

"Just give me a minute," he said, voice dwindling to a mumble as he passed out.

"Ignis?" She shook his shoulder. "Ignis, come on. We can't stay here."

His eyelashes fluttered, showing a sliver of gold. Still, he didn't wake. She yanked the cape from the chest and tossed it over him; the mist wasn't as dense inside the cabin, but it would still hurt him if he wasn't using his powers to protect himself. The pounding on the door was so loud it could've been coming from the inside of Roda's skull. Her heart slammed against her ribs in time.

Then a crash: the front door had been knocked to the ground.

She jumped to her feet. Was it another monster? What was she supposed to do now? She couldn't move Ignis, couldn't wake him, couldn't leave him behind, and couldn't outrun anything that wanted to chase her anyway. She was trapped between the slowly splintering basement door and the footsteps advancing down the hall—

A cloaked figure swung around the doorway and froze at the threshold. It wasn't a monster; it was a person. His scuffed boots took him another hesitant step forward. A gloved hand reached up to tug off his hood and pull down the scarf wrapped around the lower half of his face.

Roda's jaw dropped. The stranger had soot-colored skin and golden eyes, just like Ignis. He looked to be about Aunt Dora's age, and his hair was all white, even the stubble on his jaw. But it was undeniable: this man was another Aethon.

"I'm not going to hurt you," he said. Unconsciously, Roda had pressed back against the wall as if she meant to disappear into it. His voice was hoarse, like he hadn't spoken in days.

"Come with me," he said, inching closer. "You need to get away from there. That door won't hold."

The banging on the basement door was so loud she almost couldn't hear his words. Her eyes slid down to Ignis, passed out on the ground. The stranger must have taken that as permission, because he crossed the room and knelt down next to him.

"Who are you?" she said. And then, as he pushed the cape aside and picked Ignis up: "Don't touch him!"

"It's all right," he said. Ignis's head lolled against the man's shoulder. "Just follow me."

He stood easily and strode away. The basement door banged again; the wood bowed with the force of it. Roda flinched and pushed off the wall, following the stranger.

They walked over the front door, which was now flat on the ground. The blank all-over whiteness of the mist was almost a relief. It was quiet. Their footsteps were soft, and the noises from the cabin soon faded into the distance. The man kept glancing over his shoulder to check that she was still with him, as if he expected her to go wandering off on her own. She didn't meet his eyes.

Instead, she watched Ignis. His unconscious form crackled faintly with electricity every few moments. Was he awake? No, that wasn't it. It was the stranger. Lightning played over his features and on the sliver of skin visible between his gloves and sleeves, winding around his arms like bracelets. He was using his powers to keep the mist away from himself and Ignis both.

As the adrenaline wore off, exhaustion set in. It was well past midnight and this had been the longest day of. her life. Roda's body and mind had reached their limit.

But they still had to climb the mist. They still had a comet to catch. When Ignis woke up—*Please let that be soon*, she thought—they would keep going.

She just hoped the stranger wasn't dangerous, because she didn't have any energy left to run.

"Not too much farther," he said, as if reading her mind.

"Who are you?" she asked again, raising her voice to be heard through the scarf over her mouth. If she kept quiet any longer, she'd fall asleep on her feet. "Why are you here?"

"I'm a traveler," he said. "Just passing through."

"That's illegal."

"Is it?" He smiled charmingly. Roda was so used to Ignis by now that the fangs didn't even bother her. "My mistake."

"How did you know we needed help?"

"I didn't. But I heard strange noises," he said. "So I decided to investigate. What are *you* doing out here? You must be, what, ten years old?"

"No, twelve," she said indignantly.

"Twelve," he repeated under his breath, with a wince. "Whatever you're doing here, it's not worth it. Go home."

"I can't. My mom needs help," she said. "This is the only way I can save her."

The Traveler didn't say anything. There was something so familiar about him, but what?

The note in her pocket burned. Aethons didn't just *pass through* Brume. They were so reclusive most people didn't even know what they actually looked like. But if Anonymous knew Ignis, then that meant there was a strong possibility that Anonymous was another Aethon. Maybe *this* Aethon.

"Where are we going?" she asked.

"Someplace safe. It's hard to explain. You'll see when we—*there*."

They'd reached a grove of dead trees, all scraggly and bare and crusted over with frost. The Traveler wove between them carefully, pausing to stomp down here and there.

At last, instead of the muffled *thump* of his boot hitting the ground, there was a hollow *bang*.

"Knew it was around here somewhere," he said. "The handle's there—can you get it?"

She wiped off a layer of dirt and found a metal ring affixed to a wooden trapdoor. With a heave, she got it unstuck, and it swung open. A set of stairs led down a stone passage.

"I'll go first," the Traveler said briskly. "You'll want to shut the door behind you so we don't let the mist in."

"I can't follow a stranger into a place like that!"

Especially if you're really Anonymous, she thought.

"Fair enough," he said. "Bye, then."

And he carried Ignis down the stairs.

CH. 10

FUMING, RODA FOLLOWED, SHUTTING THE TRAPDOOR on the cold. Her flashlight turned the cracks between the stones into bottomless ravines. She ran her free hand along the wall for balance. The stairs turned once at a small landing and then descended into an open space that looked like a cross between a cave, a library, and a laboratory. Eddies of dust swirled through her light as she dragged it over every corner, trying to make sense of it all.

A pair of worktables dominated the center of the space, but their surfaces were completely obscured by bundles of paper, rolled-up scrolls, bottles containing unidentifiable congealed substances, wooden wheels with unfamiliar symbols carved into their edges. A set of rusted-over scales sat beside a pile of paper parcels containing what she assumed to be portioned ingredients that must've rotted away long ago. Nearby stood a piece of equipment made of a dozen glass chambers cobbled together, affixed to a rotating frame, and filled with sand.

One wall was crammed floor-to-ceiling with bookcases, some of the shelves bowing under the weight they bore. The wall opposite the stairs was covered in chalkboards, maps, diagrams, and scraps of paper with hurriedly scribbled notes. A desk held heaps of journals, a line of ink pots, and several quills. The chair was pushed out at an angle, as if its occupant had only just gotten up. Against the other wall stood cupboards, locked trunks, drawers, and more shelves, containing objects Roda couldn't have hoped to guess the purpose of. A pile of rich, velvety cloth had been dumped unceremoniously atop a crate. Clay pots, here and there, must have housed plants a long time ago.

The Traveler set Ignis down, propping him up against a wooden chest with brass fittings. Then he began rummaging through the cabinets.

"Now where did the old man stash the—ouch!" he said, whipping his hand away from something that threw out sparks. "Why he left all this garbage lying around, I'll never . . ."

He lifted a large bottle made of blue-green glass off the top of a shelf. When he tapped it with a finger, something burst to life inside, its glow painting cerulean shadows over the Traveler's face. He uncapped the bottle, flipped it upside down, and shook it.

A stream of thimble-sized lights popped free of the bottle and drifted into the air.

At first Roda thought they were fireflies, then stars. They filled the room like a miniature galaxy. Some floated at eye level. Others clung to the ceiling. Still more of them bobbed over the shelves, briefly illuminating cracked book spines. None were bigger than a candle's flame, but they shone far brighter and fiercer than any candle she'd ever seen.

One of them approached her with something like curiosity, drifting around her in a slow circle. She held out her hand. It floated so close that its feathery outline brushed her fingertips, though she felt nothing through her gloves. Then it darted away, skittish as a cat.

"Wow," she whispered.

"It's safe to take off your gear," the Traveler said. "Don't worry about the wisps. They're not dangerous."

"What are they?" Roda said, shedding her goggles and scarf with relief. She flicked off the flashlight, too, wanting to save it for when she'd need it again. "What's . . . all of this?"

"The wisps," said the Traveler, "were spelled into being by Aurelion Kader. I'm not sure if they were his assistants, his pets, or just a convenient substitute for candles. This place belonged to him."

He picked up the velvet cloth, shook it out, and used it to wipe the dust off the desk and chair. Once he'd cleaned to his satisfaction, he sat and pulled over a stack of journals.

"But why is it . . . here?"

This stuff belonged in museums and universities and archives, not some musty old crypt hidden away in the mist, where no one could find it.

"How much do you know about him?" the Traveler asked.

"Um," she said guiltily, recalling how her mind tended to wander during history lessons. "I know he made the mist. With an enchantment. And . . . the comet's named after him."

Maybe the secret to *climbing the mist* and *catching the comet* was here, hidden amongst Kader's belongings. But it would take her forever to sort through it all.

The Traveler glanced over at her, beginning to answer, and stopped short—as if he'd forgotten what he was going to say. Her hand rose unconsciously to her hair. Had she failed to cover up properly? But the ends, at least, were still black.

Whatever had come over the Traveler quickly passed. His expression was neutral again a moment later.

"That's a start," he said, turning back to the journal he was flipping through. "The mist was one of the greatest undertakings of his life. But his *real* specialty, what he devoted most of his research to, was understanding destiny. Professor Kader wanted to master it. Defeat it. And he *did*." He paused to take a notebook of his own out of his satchel. Ignoring the quills and the doubtless dried-out ink pots, he produced a pen from his boot. *Just like Aunt Dora*, she thought. She fought down a wave of homesickness.

When the Traveler had barged into the cabin and she'd heard those footsteps, a small, hopeful part of her had expected it to be Aunt Dora coming to her rescue. It wasn't until this moment that she realized how crushingly disappointed she felt that it hadn't been.

What if it wasn't just Mom who was in trouble? What if

something had happened to Aunt Dora, too?

No. That was impossible. Aunt Dora had survived a lot worse than this. Roda wouldn't be afraid for her. She wouldn't even entertain the thought.

"But then," the Traveler continued, "he abandoned all his research. He decided it was too dangerous to share." He copied something from Professor Kader's journal into his own notebook. "Paranoid old man. Still, he couldn't bring himself to destroy his life's work, so he hid it in bunkers like this one, all over the world. Underground time capsules full of invaluable knowledge. I've spent years tracking them all down."

He used his pen to gesture at their surroundings. "This one was the first I ever found, but I was just starting out in my research back then. I barely knew what I was looking for. The memory problems didn't help, either. So I wanted to see it one more time before . . . before the next step in my journey."

"Memory problems? Did you get hit in the head?"

"In a manner of speaking."

Roda took off her gloves and coat; it was so warm she could hardly think, let alone follow what the Traveler was saying.

"If he wanted his research left alone, then shouldn't you

respect his wishes?" she said.

She felt kind of bad for Aurelion Kader, going to such great lengths to hide his work, only for strangers like her and the Traveler to come snooping around when he was long gone and couldn't tell them to mind their own business. It was like disturbing a grave.

The Traveler scooted around in his seat to face her, using his finger to mark his spot in the journal. "What if you could save the world?" he said, his eyes shining with hope. "What if you could stop bad things from happening? *Forever.* Wouldn't you want to do that?"

"I . . . guess?" she said. Everyone wanted that, didn't they?

"Exactly!"

He bent over Kader's writings again.

She didn't have time to sit around and watch the Traveler read, but she couldn't leave without Ignis, either, and he didn't wake when she shook his shoulder. He was still out cold. With a sigh, she left him there and gave in to the urge to examine the bunker more closely. She wandered to the bookshelves first, since they were the least intimidating part of the room, and swept her finger along a row of spines. It came away black. She wiped it off on her pants, wrinkling her nose.

Soon, she tired of aimlessly sifting through texts she didn't understand and breathing in hundreds of years' worth of dust, so she plopped down next to Ignis. He'd wake up any minute now, she told herself. Then the two of them could leave this strange place and the even stranger person haunting it, before their time ran out.

If the Traveler *was* Anonymous, was it safe for her to confront him about it? He didn't seem threatening. But neither had Anonymous, at first.

Her eyes prickled with exhaustion, and her mind wandered.

"This must be hard for you," he said, after an hour of near silence. Roda jolted back into wakefulness. "Being alone out here, fearing for your family."

She suppressed a wave of emotion that threatened to overwhelm her. There would be time for feeling sad and scared *later*, once Mom was okay. Aunt Dora had never mentioned crying during *her* adventures, even when things weren't going her way.

When she looked up, the Traveler's expression was warm. She searched his face for some sign of guilt or deceit. But she found nothing. For an Aethon, he was as different from Ignis as it was possible to be: soft-spoken, calm, thoughtful. And better at masking his emotions.

"I'm not alone," she said. "I have Ignis."

"Right. I'm sure he's very helpful," the Traveler said, with a wry look at Ignis, who was still slumped under the cloak the Traveler had draped over him.

Roda bristled. "He *is* helpful. He saved both our lives."

"Really? I thought *I* did that."

"You were mistaken," she snapped.

The Traveler laughed.

"All right, I get it. You won't hear a word against your friend. Point taken." He hesitated. "What happened to your mother?"

"She's sick," Roda said. "And my aunt is missing."

"Your aunt?" he repeated. His lips parted in surprise.

"Yes," Roda said. "What?"

"You just—reminded me of something," he said. He tugged at a black cord tucked under the collar of his shirt. "Does your aunt have something that looks like this?"

He held up the end of the necklace. Dangling from the cord was an iron ring with a blue stone. It was identical to Aunt Dora's.

Roda gaped at him. "Where did you get that?"

"She has the same one, doesn't she? This aunt of yours?"

Roda said nothing. To her surprise, he dropped the necklace and covered his face with his hands. He was laughing, long and hard, almost hysterically.

"I can't believe her!" he said. "That devious little—"

He stopped. His smile faded into something sadder, pained.

"You know her," she said, sitting bolt upright.

"We've met."

"Then you have to help me find her!"

All her suspicions that the Traveler had written the letters fled her mind. He knew Aunt Dora. They had matching rings. Roda didn't know what they were for, but if it meant that Aunt Dora trusted him, then Roda could, too.

But he shook his head.

"I'm sorry," he said.

"What? Why?"

"I have something important I need to do."

"So you don't care?" Roda demanded. "I never saw Aunt Dora take off that ring, not even once. She wears it every day. Now she's gone missing, and it doesn't matter to you?"

"I care," he said, his voice strained, like it hurt to speak. "But you don't understand—"

"Maybe you should take that ring off! What's the point in wearing it if it doesn't mean anything?"

The Traveler sighed heavily. His shoulders slumped. "I probably should take it off."

But he didn't.

"Did you write those letters?" Roda asked, unable to hold back any longer.

"What letters?" he said. The journal had already seized his attention once more. He studied the open page as if it held the answers to all the questions of the universe.

"Fine," Roda said. "I don't need your help."

She pulled her knees up to her chest. They didn't speak again, and soon—though she fought against her own exhaustion, desperate to keep an eye on the clock—she drifted off to sleep, leaning against the trunk next to Ignis. Before her eyes slid shut all the way, she thought she heard the Traveler's voice, bidding her good night.

But maybe she'd only imagined that.

CH. 11

RODA WOKE TO THE SOUND OF THE TRAPDOOR SLAMMING shut.

It had the effect of a bucket of ice water dumped over her head. She was wide awake, heart hammering, already halfway to her feet before she processed what was happening.

The Traveler was gone. Beside her, Ignis stirred.

A *bang* came from the staircase, followed by a crashing like an avalanche. This lasted for several long seconds. And then there was a horrible silence.

She threw herself up to the first landing, turned the corner—and her heart plummeted. The passage had caved in; a mountain of dirt and stone blocked her way to the exit.

"Help!" she tried. Maybe . . . Maybe this had been an accident. Maybe the Traveler would come back. . . .

But her hopes were dashed when the Traveler's muffled voice replied: "I'm sorry about this. But I can't let you follow me."

"Follow you? We're not—" But she choked on the words. "You're going to the top of the mist."

"If you somehow get out before the comet passes," he said, "and if I see you . . . I'll do whatever it takes to stop you."

"But why?" she shouted.

No answer. Panic welled up in her chest.

"Come back! *Please!* You can't leave us here!"

But he was gone.

Behind her, Ignis shrieked. Roda sprinted back down the stairs, only to find him swatting at the wisps. There were about a dozen of them crowding him in the spirit of investigation. His other arm covered his face, but Roda couldn't tell whether it was because of the brightness of the wisps or because he was worried one of them was going to fly up his nose.

"What *are* these things and *why* are they in my space?" he demanded. "And who does this ratty cloak belong to and where *are* we?"

"We're *trapped* is where we are," she fumed. That put an end to her theory that the Traveler was Anonymous. He was actively stopping them from doing what Anonymous wanted.

She told Ignis what had happened after he'd passed out. Ignis's eyes practically popped out of his head.

"And you just let him leave?"

"What else was I supposed to do?"

"Anything other than fall *asleep*."

She didn't want to admit that the reason why she'd let her guard down around the Traveler was because of his connection to Aunt Dora. And she didn't want to bring up the matching rings. It felt too much like gossiping.

"*You're* one to talk!" she said instead. "You slept for—"

Suddenly terrified they'd wasted the whole day, she checked her pocket watch and breathed a sigh of relief that it was still morning. They had until eleven o'clock that evening, when Kader's Comet crossed the sky for the second night in a row, to figure out how to climb the mist.

But they had no idea how long the climb would take. What if it was already too late?

Don't think about that, she told herself.

"Never mind," Ignis said. "He's gone. What do we do now?"

"We need to find a way out."

They tried digging to the exit and got nothing for it but scraped hands and dirt under their fingernails. With every inch of progress they made, more of the walls loosened and collapsed.

"Stop," Ignis said at last. "This whole passage might be unstable now. We could bring the roof down on our heads."

They took a break to eat some of the food Roda had packed. Once they got their energy up, they could search the rest of the bunker.

"If he wanted to stop us so bad, why didn't he let that thing in the cabin kill us?" she asked, thinking aloud. Nothing the Traveler had done made any sense to her.

Ignis grimaced. "I can't believe there are spirit-hoarders in this place."

"Spirit-hoarders?"

"They're creatures who collect souls," he said. "I should've known when I saw its nest, but it cornered me before I could get out."

"Oh," she said. She hadn't known such a horrible thing could exist. "Thanks for helping me get out of there."

The memory of claws wrapping around her ankle was still fresh enough to make her shiver. Ignis could've left her then, but he hadn't. He'd risked his life making sure they both escaped.

"You came back for me first." He shrugged.

There was a faint hissing sound, like steam rising off a kettle. A wisp that had been hiding in her collar emerged now to hover between her and Ignis.

"If Anonymous is so good at telling the future, why didn't they write you a note that said, *Dear Roda, don't trust strange men in the mist*?" Ignis complained. "Or maybe, *Dear Roda, don't shout at your friends*. Then we'd never have ended up in the cabin at all."

"Or they could've written, *Dear Ignis, don't be such a stuck-up jerk*."

"So you've finally come to the conclusion that I'm *not* the one writing the letters?" Ignis said, feigning shock. "Or, in this scenario, am I calling *myself* a jerk?"

"I know you didn't write them," she admitted. "I shouldn't have said that."

She expected an *I told you so*, but instead, Ignis looked away.

"You weren't completely wrong," he said. "There's something I haven't been telling you. It's not about the letters. It's something else."

"What?"

"I . . ." He sighed. "I lied when I said I couldn't remember anything."

Yesterday, that confession would've made her angry. Now, all she could think was that he must have had a good reason for hiding something like that.

"Why didn't you say something?" she asked, without rancor.

"I didn't . . . I didn't know what to do. I didn't have anywhere else to go," he said. "And I didn't want to talk about what happened."

She waited for him to meet her eyes before she spoke again. "Can you talk about it now?"

It took him a few minutes to find the words.

"I lived in an eyrie far north of here," he said. "With my flock. We've lived there for centuries, mostly in peace, except for the occasional clash with our enemies, the Jaculus horde that claims the mountains as their territory." A flash of hatred crossed his face for an instant before he composed himself.

"Jaculus?" she repeated, testing out the unfamiliar word. "Are they shapeshifters, too?"

"No. They have armored skin and demon eyes, and they don't know how to change shape, or fly, or do anything but fight." His shoulders tightened, like if he'd had his wings just then, they'd be fanned out in agitation. "They're so good at fighting that hardly anyone stands a chance fighting back. We defended ourselves well, but one of these conflicts . . . escalated. I don't know what happened. This time, they weren't content to pick off our border guards. They invaded, attacked—and we lost. The eyrie was brought down. It's in ruins somewhere at the base of the mountains now."

Even the wisp seemed dim and subdued after that.

"Ignis, I'm so sorry," she said.

"I escaped. Mostly because one of the guards snuck me out. He told me to fly away, so I did. I wandered for a few days, scavenging for food, and then I crashed. And that's when you found me."

"Your parents?" she asked.

"Gone. My siblings, too. They all—"

His voice broke, and he shut his mouth, scowling in a determined sort of way, like if he didn't scowl, he'd cry instead. She steered the conversation toward safer waters.

"If you remember everything, then why are you coming with me now?"

"Think about it," he said, brightening. "I grew up in the eyrie. I never left, and no one outside knew me. There are other Aethons, but they live in distant lands and keep to themselves, like we did. So whoever wrote those letters *must* be from my flock. Another survivor. Maybe even one of my relatives. I suspected it from the start, and now you're saying you just *happened* to meet another Aethon here in the mist? That's not a coincidence. If the Traveler isn't Anonymous, he still has to know more than he's letting on."

"But Anonymous was writing to me for months before we met. Before . . . what happened at the eyrie," she said. "If you're family, why wouldn't Anonymous just talk to *you*?"

"I don't know, but I'm planning to find out," he said, undaunted. "Let's keep looking."

She got to her feet and dusted off her clothes, dislodging the wisp from her shoulder.

"*You* don't know how to get out of here, do you?" Roda said to it.

"There's no way that thing—" Ignis started. His teeth clamped shut around the end of the sentence as all the wisps converged on them.

CH. 12

THE WISPS DROPPED, FLOATED, AND ZOOMED ACROSS THE bunker to surround them. There were dozens, maybe upward of a hundred, all hovering tensely in place.

"What are they doing?" Roda whispered, shielding her eyes from their glow.

"I don't know," Ignis said. "And I don't like it."

When Roda walked away, half of them trailed after her like a cape; the other half stuck with Ignis. He gave a flick of his hand, sending out a whip of lightning that made them scatter. But they returned a moment later, bobbing around his shoulders.

"It's like they're waiting for something," Roda said. Scanning the room for ideas, her eyes landed on the glass bottle where the Traveler had found them. She had to drag the desk chair over and stand on it to reach the bottle from the top shelf, and then she clutched it in both hands as she hopped down. It was heavier than it looked. A ripple went through the wisps as she examined it.

"What?" she said, glancing up at them. "Is this what you wanted me to do?"

But they gave her no more clues. She sighed, almost wishing for another letter from Anonymous.

Almost.

She turned the bottle over in her hands. The glass was warped in places, as if someone had tried to melt it.

"Why go to the trouble of making an army of magical assistants and then shove them away inside that piece of junk?" Ignis said. He almost sounded offended on the wisps' behalf.

"You're right," Roda muttered. "It's weird."

She held the bottle up to her face and peered down the opening with one eye.

Wait.

"There's something in here!" she said.

"What?"

"It's . . . There are all these cracks. . . ."

"So it's broken?"

The wisps' light seeped through the blue-green glass and highlighted the thin, almost imperceptible network of cracks mapped across the inside. They didn't radiate or form spiderwebs like normal cracks did; they had a strange, deliberate pattern to them, as if someone had put them there on purpose.

She tried to explain this to Ignis.

"Let me see," he said, grabbing it.

"*Wait*, I'm still *looking*," she complained, not letting go.

"Oh, come on. You're taking forever."

"I can almost see it—"

And that was when the bottle slipped from their fingers and crashed to the ground. Glass flew in every direction; her arms rose instinctively to cover her face. When she peeked out at the wreckage, she groaned. The bottle had shattered completely. None of the surviving pieces could've been more than an inch long, and they'd splashed everywhere, some wedged in the gaps between the stone tiles and others under the table and still more glittering from beneath the bookcases on the other end of the room.

"You broke it!" she snapped at Ignis.

"*We*," he said haughtily. "*We* broke it."

Before she could retort, another ripple went through the wisps. They scattered, diving to pick up the glass pieces.

They collected all the shards, from the largest chunks to the tiniest specks of shining dust, and slowly reassembled them into a recognizable shape.

But they weren't making a bottle. They were making a huge glass key.

She and Ignis watched in awed silence until Ignis said: "See? Isn't it lucky I thought to break it?"

"Shut *up*."

She knelt to pick up the key. There hadn't been a keyhole in the trapdoor, and there were no other doors in the bunker. Were they supposed to go around breaking things until another exit appeared?

Don't give Ignis any ideas, she told herself. He'd actually do it.

"How do we use this?" Ignis said to the wisps.

He was met with silence.

"Where is the way out?" he tried.

Still nothing. A shiver passed through the wisps.

"What's the point of a key without a lock?" he snapped, on the verge of losing his temper.

"There *has* to be one, somewhere." She laid the glass key on Kader's desk. "Help me look."

They did a circuit of the room, checking for loose stones in the walls, moving cabinets, pulling down books at random in hopes one of them would make the shelves swing aside and reveal a hidden passage. And they wound up right back where they'd started: in front of the motionless wisps, in possession of a key and no keyhole.

"We just turned the whole place over," Ignis told the wisps. "No doors. No giant glass locks. Would it kill you to give us a clue?"

He batted a mountain of ribbon-bound scrolls off the corner of a worktable and sat there, one knee pulled up, looking so much like a cranky crow with his hair still ruffled from sleep that she almost laughed.

Then it hit her. "Ignis, wait. The tables."

That was the one place they hadn't looked. Together, they cleared the tables off and shoved them to the side. There was nothing under the first one. But when they moved the second, they heard the rattle of a wobbly tile. It had been pinned in place under the table leg. Ignis lifted it up, and there it was: a keyhole set into a pane of blue-green glass.

Roda hefted their key with both hands and slid it home. The cluster of wisps exploded apart and flew into the wall like shrapnel. They lined themselves up around the sideboards and shelves in a meandering path to the ceiling. Where they touched the wall, the stone melted away, revealing a staircase carved into the side of the bunker. At the top, a final wisp brushed the ceiling, and an opening appeared. The stone simply faded away as if it had never been there. Mist drifted languidly inside—she never thought she'd be relieved to see it, but she was.

"Professor Kader was a genius," Roda said, amazed.

"A mad genius, maybe." Ignis tested out the first step. "Feels stable."

I can't wait to tell Aunt Dora about this, she thought, until she remembered she didn't know where Aunt Dora was or if she'd ever see her again. If she'd ever get to ask her about the ring and how she knew the Traveler.

She decided, then and there, to stop clinging to the hope that Aunt Dora would turn up out of the blue and save the day. Maybe she *would*, but until it happened, Roda had to accept that it was up to her and Ignis to find Anonymous and rescue Mom. No one else. She had to be strong enough to do this with or without Aunt Dora's help.

With her gear back on, she took a last look around the bunker. Then she and Ignis climbed the stairs. They were narrow and steep, and sometimes they had to walk over the tops of shelves, knocking their contents to the floor, to cross between sections. She winced every time she heard something shatter, wondering whether they'd just destroyed a priceless historical relic. But she gritted her teeth, kept her back to the wall, and inched onward. Finally, they made it to the top. With a boost from Ignis, she managed to heave herself over the edge of the opening. She pulled him up after her. The wisps filtered out, too, as if they'd had enough of waiting around for Professor Kader to return. They dispersed into the mist, golden droplets of light swallowed up by a milky white sea. All except for one, which tucked itself into the folds of her scarf.

As soon as she and Ignis were clear, the opening disappeared. There was a distant rumble, like the growl of some immense beast. At first, she thought it was coming from the bunker beneath them.

"What *is* that?" Ignis asked. She strained her ears.

The ground trembled. A piercing whistle cut through the air. It wasn't coming from the bunker. She *knew* that sound—every human being in the Aerlands knew it.

Through the mist, a powerful light beamed down on them, half blinding her.

She looked down. Her heart stopped as she realized what they were standing on.

CH. 13

SHE GRABBED IGNIS AND THREW HERSELF OFF THE TRAIN tracks, sending them both sprawling. The rumble swelled to a deafening roar. All at once, the train blasted into view, parting the mist like a knife. It sped over the tracks with such strength and power that she and Ignis, inches from the blur of its passing bulk, were nearly blown away by a surge of wind. Even through her coverings, she coughed at the overpowering smell of engine oil.

Beside her, Ignis's eyes were wide. The wisp had fallen out of Roda's scarf and clung now to a lock of his hair.

Then the train passed, vanishing into the outer reaches of the mist and beyond. Her ears rang. It took a few seconds before she could hear her own breathing again.

"What was that?" Ignis asked shakily.

"A train. They . . . they take you through the mist and all over the Aerlands," she said. "Sometimes monsters try to attack them, but they can't, because—"

She stopped. There was someone standing on the other side of the tracks. She and Ignis got to their feet.

"Should we run?" Ignis asked, lips barely moving, not taking his eyes off the figure.

She shook her head, too awed to speak.

The silhouette beside the tracks was giant-sized, at least three times a grown man's height. It faced the direction the train had gone, as if watching it depart, but at the sound of their voices, it turned.

There was nothing but a beaming headlight where its face should have been. The golden light shot straight across the tracks, through the mist, and bathed them in its harsh glow. The wisp hid behind Ignis.

"Is he a god?" Ignis asked in a strained whisper.

"It's okay," she finally managed. "That's one of the train guardians."

"YOU DO NOT BELONG HERE," said the automaton, in a colossal rumble of a voice. It rang through her bones and thrummed through the ground under her feet; she held her breath until the sound died away.

The guardian stepped over the train tracks in one stride. As he approached—it felt rude to keep calling a speaking, sentient being *it*, even though automatons didn't particularly care what they were called—his features became clearer: the boulder-like head and great drum-shaped torso, tree trunk-sized arms that ended in three-fingered hands. With every step he took, his casing flashed in the weak, filtered sunlight, and his joints creaked noisily. Ignis winced and made as if to clap his hands over his ears, but Roda grabbed his arm to still him. The last thing she wanted to do was offend the train guardian.

The guardians were remnants of a long-lost civilization from a time before the mist existed. Back then, they'd been warriors who fought alongside human soldiers against the monsters that ravaged the Aerlands. Now, they defended the trains during their treacherous journeys.

The secret to building the guardians was lost. Every train guardian who still existed had been "alive" for centuries. With none of their original creators around to care for them, they stopped functioning one by one, and fewer trains ran between the Aerlands' cities. Once, a train guardian had malfunctioned mid-journey; the passengers were left without protection, and a horde of wyverns had attacked. The result had been catastrophic.

The guardian looming over them now was older than the mist. Older than Roda's entire world, basically.

"Hello," Roda said, in a very small voice.

He peered down at her with his one eye like a spotlight. Squinting, she craned her neck all the way back to see his face. But Ignis backed away, dragging her along by the elbow.

"Stop that!" she hissed.

"That thing could *stomp us to death*," he whispered back.

"Hello," she said again, shaking him off. "I'm Roda. It's nice to meet you."

She held out her hand. Ignis made a noise of disbelief in the back of his throat, but the guardian reached out and offered one of his three club-like fingers for her to shake.

"**I AM TRAX**," he boomed. "**I LOOK AFTER THE TRAINS. YOU DO NOT BELONG HERE.**"

She was on a first-name basis with a train guardian. Aunt Dora would be *so* jealous.

"We're trying to climb *up* the mist," she said awkwardly. It sounded so ridiculous when she said it aloud. "Is that . . . possible?"

"**YES**," he said.

"Oh!" Roda could hardly believe it. "How?"

"YOU MUST PAY THE FARE."

"Pay?" she repeated. Of all the essentials she'd thought to pack, money hadn't been one of them. "Okay. Okay, wait."

She dug around in her bag for anything remotely valuable. The pocket watch might work, but she needed it to keep track of how much time they had left until Kader's Comet.

Ignis tapped on her shoulder insistently. When she looked up, he was holding out a shiny gold coin.

"Is that . . . from the spirit-hoarder's nest?" she asked, exasperated and impressed in equal measures.

He grinned. "It might be."

"Ignis! When did you have time to steal?"

"It's not really stealing if *they* stole it first," he said. He offered the coin to Trax. "Is this okay?"

"IT IS SUFFICIENT," Trax said. He accepted the coin and opened a compartment in the place where his stomach would've been. The door was affixed with a dial that turned like a safe. When he deposited the coin inside, they caught a glimpse of his trove, which included coins, bills, jewelry, feathers, and an assortment of objects Roda didn't have time to identify. He plucked a small piece of paper from the collection, withdrew his hand, and sealed the compartment shut.

He presented the paper to Roda. For a wild second, she expected it to be a ticket of some kind, as if they were about to embark on a sky train. But it wasn't a ticket. It was a note.

You're running out of time. Climb fast.

"Who gave this to you?" she asked, voice shaking.

"A PASSENGER," Trax replied.

"Yes, but—*who* was the passenger? What was their name—what did they look like—?"

Trax tilted his head to the side, as if he didn't understand the question. "**PASSENGER**," he said again.

She looked at Ignis, who shook his head.

"Forget it," she said, pocketing the note. "What now?"

Trax reached up, stretching to his full height. His hand disappeared into the mist and grabbed hold of something twenty feet in the air, well out of sight.

And he *pulled*.

Roda clapped a hand over her mouth to hold back a scream. His enormous fingers clutched the end of a scaly, reptilian tail, which curled around his hand, alive.

The white scales gleamed under Trax's headlight. The

end of the tail was thin enough for Trax to wrap his fingers around. Higher up, it widened, and a spiky, pale blue ridge ran along its back.

She couldn't see what the tail was attached to. This creature had been hovering over them all this time, and they'd had no idea.

"Those are dragon scales," Ignis said, leaning over Trax's outstretched hand to study the tail up close. "Look at how sharp the edges are, and how they're overlapping. They lie smooth when the dragon's calm, but when it needs to fight or defend itself, they stand on end. It's like its whole body is covered with razors."

"Dragon?" she repeated faintly. "There's a dragon in the mist?"

"THE DRAGON *IS* THE MIST," Trax said.

"But . . ." Roda said. Dragons were supposed to be extinct. "How?"

She blurted out the question without really expecting an answer this time, so she was caught off guard when Trax responded:

"SECRETS HAVE A PRICE. WHAT WILL YOU PAY?"

"Will you trade one secret for another?" Ignis asked. Trax nodded creakily.

"I don't know if I have any," Roda said. The biggest secret she'd ever kept was Ignis.

"I have one," he said, and took a deep breath. "When my home was attacked, I didn't fight back, even though I've been taking combat lessons almost my whole life. It turned out I couldn't handle a *real* fight. I panicked. I couldn't save anyone. I just ran away. It's the most shameful thing I've ever done."

His voice betrayed no emotion, but Roda knew what it must have cost him to say such a thing out loud.

"I thought of one, too," she said, surprising herself as much as Ignis. "I'm afraid Anonymous targeted me because they somehow knew I'd be easy to fool. That I was bored with my life, so when something exciting finally happened to me, I'd ignore all the warning signs that told me Anonymous was dangerous. I'm afraid what happened to Mom is *my* fault."

She'd barely realized she felt that way until the words were out of her mouth. Regret burned in the back of her throat. Through the goggles, she met Ignis's eyes and knew, without him saying anything, that he understood.

"THEN HERE IS A SECRET FOR YOU. LONG AGO," Trax said, **"A HUMAN MAGE PLACED THE ICE DRAGONS OF THE AERLANDS IN**

AN ENCHANTED SLEEP. HE WRAPPED THEM AROUND YOUR CITIES AND TOWNS FOR PROTECTION. AND THEY HAVE REMAINED THERE EVER SINCE."

She'd known about Aurelion Kader's enchantment. Everyone did. But she'd thought the mist *was* the enchantment. She'd never heard anything about dragons or a sleeping spell.

"THIS DRAGON SLEEPS AS IT HAS SLEPT FOR ALL THESE YEARS: WITH ITS TAIL BRUSHING THE GROUND AND ITS NOSE IN THE SKY," Trax said. "ITS RESTING BODY COILS AROUND AND AROUND IN A SPIRAL TOWER. THE MIST COMES FROM ITS SCALES."

Sure enough, delicate tendrils of mist drifted off the pearly scales in Trax's hand.

"WHEN IT FLIES, IT PASSES FOR A CLOUD," Trax said. "BUT THIS DRAGON WILL NOT FLY AGAIN FOR A VERY LONG TIME. YOU MAY PROCEED."

"Proceed where?" Roda said, and then the horrible truth struck her. "We have to climb up the dragon?"

"IT SLEEPS."

"I know, but—"

Roda didn't know how to explain to a centuries-old

automaton why prancing around on a dragon's back wasn't appealing in the slightest, whether it was asleep or awake.

"We don't have a choice, do we?" Ignis said. "It's not like we're turning back now."

He stepped onto the dragon's tail while Trax held it steady, balancing carefully until he'd walked up to where its tail broadened and its back ridge grew tall enough for him to hold on to like a rail. Her stomach swooped as she watched him ascend. If he slipped down here it wouldn't matter, but what would happen when they were fifty feet in the air? One hundred feet? What would happen when they were at the top of the mist, high enough, if Anonymous was correct, to catch hold of a comet?

And what would happen if they ran into the Traveler on their way up?

I'll do whatever it takes to stop you.

"Come on!" Ignis called, bouncing impatiently on the balls of his feet.

Roda took a deep, calming breath. He was right. There was no going back. All she was doing by hesitating was wasting time, which, as Anonymous had just reminded her, she couldn't afford to do.

And if she survived this, maybe *she'd* have a story to tell Aunt Dora, for once, instead of the other way around.

"Thank you, Trax," she said.

She placed her boot on the dragon's tail and stepped off the ground.

Her footsteps made a faint crackling sound like they were pressing down on ice. The mist obscured the ground in seconds. It became impossible to tell how high up she was. The sky, too, was well out of sight. Roda had nothing but the shimmering white path of scales to guide her.

Ignis raced ahead of her, so she kept losing track of him.

"Wait up!" she called. If she slipped and fell to her death, she wanted a witness. Other than the wisp, which had affixed itself to her collar again.

Ignis returned, skidding down the slope of the dragon's back. She felt unsteady just watching him.

"You should be careful."

"I can fly, remember?" he said, walking backward in front of her.

"Don't rub it in," she grumbled. "Some of us have never been this high up."

"This is nothing. I wish you could've seen the eyrie."

He grinned, but it faded fast.

"Tell me about it." She summoned an encouraging smile. "I bet it was amazing. It'll take my mind off the climb."

Roda didn't know anything about grief. She'd never lost anyone close to her, except her dad, but she didn't remember him enough to miss him. And Mom—she hadn't lost her yet. Mom could still be saved.

Would be saved.

How much worse would she feel right now, without hope? If all had already been lost?

She suspected that Ignis needed to talk about it, after keeping his secret for so long. Maybe it would do him some good to finally share.

"Imagine the tallest mountain in the world," he said, his eyes distant and dreamy, "and at the peak of the mountain, there's a tower. You could stand on top of it and touch the moon. Lightning rains down from this tower and turns midnight to gold. That's where we lived."

Time passed quickly as Roda focused on Ignis's voice. She asked questions when he paused for breath but mostly stayed quiet, letting the tales of his childhood distract her from the knowledge that every step took her farther and farther from the ground. During the exciting parts— like the story of when Ignis had first learned to fly as a fledgling and crash-landed into rock-giant territory—the wisp fluttered around his head, as if impatient to hear what happened next.

Step by step, they rose through the mist.

CH. 14

THEY STOPPED BRIEFLY IN THE AFTERNOON TO REST AND eat. The delay made her nervous, but they'd never make it to the top if they passed out from hunger.

Ignis sat down with his back against the dragon's spinal ridge. The ridge was made up of eight-foot-tall spikes, frosty blue like glacier ice, which were connected to each other by some kind of hard webbing. She'd spent the climb running her hand along it for balance, even though it was so cold her palm had gone numb through her glove.

Carefully, she sank down beside Ignis, slipped, and fell on her bottom with a yelp. Ignis grabbed her shoulder to steady her.

"Calm down!" he said. "You're nowhere near the edge.

Besides, I *told* you, in an emergency I'm sure I could catch you. I've never flown with another person before, but I know I could do that much."

He really had a lot of faith in his crow form's strength. Before she could retort, a whisper of a voice spoke straight into her ear.

"Calm."

She jumped. But there was no one next to her. Only the wisp.

"You spoke!"

"Me?" Ignis said.

"No!" She gestured at the wisp. "You can talk?"

It trembled, as if struggling.

"Learning," it said at last, in a ghost of a voice, raspy and indistinct.

This time, Ignis heard, too.

"Learning?" he said. "From us?"

"Remembering."

"That's amazing!" Roda said. She held out her hands, inviting the wisp to sink into the cup of her palms. "What's your name?"

It made a series of incomprehensible hissing and crackling noises.

"I'm Roda," she replied. "And this is Ignis."

"*Roda.*" It lengthened the first syllable into a breathy *whoosh* and clipped the second short: *Rooooh-da.*

"That's right!" she said encouragingly. "What if we gave you a nickname?"

Ignis rolled his eyes. But the wisp bounced excitedly.

"All right, let me think," she said. "May we call you Will?"

The wisp did a little twirl in the air, which looked like a *yes* to her.

"I can't believe you're naming the thing that tried to kill us," Ignis said. "Like it's your pet."

"They weren't trying to kill us," Roda said. "How could the wisps have known about the train? The tracks wouldn't have been there in Kader's time."

"It's magic," Ignis said. "How do *you* know they didn't know?"

Roda frowned, and then she shook her head. "I'm choosing to believe it. Either way, if it can learn to talk, then it can learn to be good."

"You're too trusting."

"If I weren't," she said, "I would've ignored Anonymous's notes and kicked you out as soon as I realized you weren't a crow."

"And maybe you would've been better off for it," he said quietly.

"No. I don't think I would've been."

Not too long ago, in a fit of frustration, she'd thought that Ignis brought out the worst in her. Maybe that was true. But Ignis also made her braver.

They fell silent. The thought of the climb ahead turned the food to chalk in her mouth, but she finished her rations determinedly. She couldn't afford to lose energy now.

"Have you thought about what happens when we reach the top?" he asked, brushing crumbs off his hands.

She tugged out the note she'd found with Mom, unfolded it, and read it again.

"I thought the instructions didn't make sense," she said, "but they did. It means exactly what it says. The mist really *can* be climbed. So that means . . ."

"When Anonymous says to catch the comet, they mean it literally," he finished. She nodded and pulled the other letters out of her bag.

"Look at these," she said. "The older notes started with riddles—I *thought* they were riddles, anyway. Now I'm not so sure."

He took the notes from her and scanned them.

"'A place you can only enter through one door, but can leave through many,'" he read aloud. "'A place you must either leave in ten seconds or stay for ten years. An engine that never runs out of fuel . . .'"

"Then it says, *nowhere*. But why tell me about a place that doesn't exist? Unless *nowhere* isn't just an answer to the question. What if it's a *name*?"

He peered up at her over the notes, a crease between his eyebrows.

"A place called Nowhere?"

"It says here to *open the door*," Roda said, scooting closer and jabbing at one of the notes. Will drifted in circles around their heads, as if wondering what all the fuss was about. "And in the other letter, it says, 'you can only enter through one door.' Maybe both these letters are talking about the same door. The door to Nowhere."

"If that's true," he said, "then the rest of it must be true. We could get stuck there for ten years."

She faltered. "Not if we leave in ten seconds."

"There's no way Anonymous dragged us up here just to send us away after ten seconds," he said.

She leaned back, staring blankly out into the mist. What none of the notes said was *why*. Why did Anonymous want her to do any of this? What would happen when they met face-to-face?

The prospect of seeing the Traveler again made her nervous, too. He'd talked about saving the world, and then he'd locked her and Ignis in a basement. His parting threat still echoed in her mind. She didn't know what to think, other than to wonder how he was connected to Anonymous, and to wherever they were going. Because it all *had* to be connected.

All this time, Roda had thought of Anonymous as being *hers*, in a way: her correspondent, her friend, and then her enemy. And Ignis had thought Anonymous was a link to his lost family, a chance to meet another survivor. But maybe they were both wrong. Maybe Anonymous was tied to something much bigger than either of them.

"There has to be more to it than that," she said. "We're missing something."

"Probably," Ignis said. He slipped the notes back into her bag, and Will settled down in her scarf. "We need a plan for when we get to the top. Any idea how we're supposed to catch a comet?"

"Maybe it'll be obvious when we get there," she said, without enthusiasm. "When we got to the dragon, that was obvious."

"But we wandered around for ages first," he pointed out. "We won't have that kind of time. We'll only have—"

"Ten seconds," she said, as her stomach gave a queasy jolt.

Ignis met her worried gaze with a look of grim determination.

"We'll only have one chance to get it right. How do you want to do this?"

"I don't know," she admitted.

"I think I do," he said. "Why do you think Anonymous wanted to make sure you found me?"

Roda shook her head helplessly. Everything was a confusing mess.

"I can *fly*," Ignis said. "Pretty helpful to be able to fly when you're trying to catch hold of a comet. Don't you think?"

"You want to fly us up?" she said. She pulled at a loose thread on the sleeve of her coat, unable to meet his eyes.

"I know you're scared of heights and you don't think I can carry us both—"

"I never said that."

"—but I *can*. I promise."

"But—"

"I can do it. Just trust me. Do you?"

She stopped picking at her sleeve and finally looked at him. There was no trace of doubt on his face.

"I do trust you," she said.

He bared his sharp teeth in a grin. "Good. Then let's go."

CH. 15

RODA DIDN'T KNOW HOW HIGH UP THEY WERE ANYMORE. At least halfway, she hoped. It had been hours. The daylight had dulled to a subdued gold that stained the mist in shades of amber and honey. But checking her watch for the millionth time wouldn't make the two of them go any faster, so she forced herself to put it out of her mind and focus only on the next step.

Her boot came down on the slippery-smooth surface of the dragon's hide, and something brushed against her heel.

She yelped. Will jumped away from her, flickering nervously; Ignis, a short way ahead, turned back.

"What?"

"It *moved*."

"I didn't feel anything."

Tentatively, she fanned away some of the mist with her gloved hand, squinting through her goggles at the last place she'd stepped.

"Oh," she said. "It wasn't the dragon."

Ignis doubled back to join her and crouched down. "That's—ugh. Gross."

"*Gross*," Will agreed, settling on Ignis's shoulder.

"What is it?" Roda asked quietly, not wanting to spook the small creature. It was sleek and limbless, wormlike; bony plating protected its head and upper body, but its back and tail were bright blue. Its skin was faintly translucent, so that she could see through to its skeleton. As they watched, it nibbled along the edge of a scale, its hovering body undulating with the currents of the mist. Its flat eyes rolled up as if to examine them in return.

"Don't know. It looks like it's eating the dead cells on the edge of the scales," Ignis said. "Dragon scales grow, just like hair and nails. I guess these . . . cleaners keep them trimmed and sharp."

Will floated next to it curiously. It twitched toward him, almost bumping him with its nose, and he made a hasty retreat.

There were even more of the creatures—the *cleaners*—higher up, none larger than Roda's shoe, and all far too busy to acknowledge Ignis's and Roda's existence. A dragon this size required round-the-clock scale maintenance, it seemed.

As they ascended, the chill burrowed through her thick layers and seeped into her skin. The air grew thinner and harder to breathe. She panted as they climbed higher and higher, her gloved hand trailing along the spinal ridge. More and more, she was leaning against the ridge for support instead of just using it to steady herself.

"I'm tired," Ignis announced at last. "Let's sit down for a few minutes."

He wasn't tired at all, and they both knew it. But she didn't argue.

No more breaks, she told herself, catching her breath. She willed herself to be strong, for Mom. Their time was running short. *After this, you keep going until the end.*

The mist swirled dark orange and pink. The sun was setting; very soon, it would be night. Dread swelled in her chest at the reminder of how close they were to the comet, and to the next, treacherous step of their journey.

Then a gust of wind made the mist part in front of her, and she caught her first glimpse of the outside world. She gasped aloud.

Spread out before her, far below, was an emerald land-scape, latticed by train tracks and dotted with towers of mist that marked where other cities lay. She could even see what must be Vicentia, the capital, to the north: a billow-ing plume of cloud so broad it could have swallowed her own town ten times over. The thought that each of those towers concealed sleeping dragons made her light-headed with a mixture of awe and fear. Even at a distance, the sheer size of them was almost too much for her mind to comprehend.

Aunt Dora had always said that the Aerlands was the most beautiful country in the whole world, and though Roda had nothing to compare it to, she was certain Aunt Dora had to be right. It was. Especially at that moment, with the sun sinking below the horizon. She'd seen paint-ings of sunsets, but she hadn't realized how *big* the sun could look, or how it bled colors she'd never even seen before.

She watched, breathless, until the wind shifted again, and the mist closed over them once more.

The sun's retreat plunged them into darkness. It wasn't a gradual shift, a slow buildup of shadow. The last traces of light just dribbled out of the mist like dye washing out of linen. Even with Will around, she couldn't see her own feet. She took out her flashlight.

Soon, the smell of smoke ambushed them. Nothing in the mist should've been capable of producing smoke, other than the trains, and they were much too far from the ground to be catching a whiff of exhaust.

"Do you hear that?" Ignis breathed.

Roda strained her ears and picked up on a rasp, a snuffle, and a billowing like a flag in the wind. Through the veil of mist, her flashlight revealed a hulking silhouette up ahead. Far too close for comfort.

She sucked in her breath, adrenaline zinging through her body, and covered the flashlight to hide its glare. Will darted behind her shoulder. Moonlight soaked into the mist, creating a soft, ambient glow, not bright enough to truly see by.

"Do you think it noticed us?" she whispered.

They held their breath, listening, but the noises didn't come any closer.

"We can't stay here," he said.

She thought of Mom, and her resolve steadied. "You're right. Come on."

Her flashlight pierced through the gaps in the mist, and as they approached, the creature swam into view: it was one of the cleaners. But *huge*. Wolf-sized, where the rest had been mice. Its undulating body hung low to the dragon's hide. She hadn't really been able to see the mouths on the other cleaners, they were so tiny. It turned out they had teeth. The cleaner's mouth protruded from its body, its jaw jutting out and lined with a bed of grinding molars. It gnawed at a patch of blackened scales—the source of the burnt smell they'd picked up earlier.

"*Gross*," Will declared in an emphatic whisper.

"Let's fly over it," Ignis said, hushed.

Roda hesitated, just about ready to agree, when a flicker of movement caught her eye. One of the tiny cleaners darted past her feet, propelling itself forward with its wriggling tail, homing in on the feast of crispy scales laid out before it.

The big cleaner made a shockingly fast move, like a viper. It whipped around and snapped the little one up. Delicate bones crunched in its boulder-like teeth.

"What if it eats birds, too?" she said, cringing. Will shrank into her collar.

One of its flat, beady eyes swiveled up to point at them. It detached itself from the scorched scales and drifted closer to them, slow, perhaps still deciding whether they were edible.

Ignis went pale. "Retreat?"

"We can't!"

But it must have decided they had come too close to its meal. It shot forward, jaws gnashing. Roda and Ignis jumped apart; it dove between them, made a sinuous figure-eight turn, and sprang at Ignis. He dodged narrowly and flung out his hand. A zap of lightning struck it between the eyes. It made a horrible, high-pitched noise, like a screech, and lunged at him again.

"Do something!" he shouted over its head, at Roda.

"Change and fly away!"

"Then it'll just go after *you*!"

Inspiration struck her. Hurriedly, she produced the last of their food. As the cleaner chased Ignis uphill, Roda tossed an apple at its tail. It whipped around to see what had smacked it. The apple disappeared between its jaws, accompanied by wet crunching noises that made her stomach churn.

Its eyes slid up to Roda, shiny and vacant, with a machinelike coldness.

With shaking fingers, she tossed the rest of the food as far from herself as she could without sending it sailing to the ground. The cleaner swooped around, tail flicking, and followed it, half slithering and half floating. Roda slipped past while it was occupied and fled with Ignis.

When the panic had faded, they stumbled to a halt.

Despite the lingering fear and the burn in her lungs, a giddy relief swept through her. Ignis hadn't needed to save her this time. *She* had saved them both.

Aunt Dora would've been so proud of her if she could've seen.

"That mark on the ground," Ignis said. "The black spot where the scales were singed. You know what that was?"

"What?" she said, panting. Her lungs squeezed, struggling to wring every last bit of oxygen from the thin air.

"A scorch mark from a lightning strike," he said. "The Traveler must have done that. On purpose, I bet. He must have known damage like that would attract a big cleaner, and he wanted to slow us down. Or worse."

"He'll probably be up there," she said uneasily. "What do you think he'll do when he sees us?"

Ignis just shook his head.

But they couldn't stop to speculate or plan. Their time was ticking away.

With two hours left until Kader's Comet, there was still no sign that the end of the climb was near. With one hour to go, Ignis insisted they run.

"We've got to be close now," he said. "It'll be over faster this way."

Roda's hands were cold and clammy even in her gloves. "I can't." Her voice was as thin as the air. "I'll slip and fall. I *know* I will."

He offered his hand. "Just hold on to me. Neither of us will fall, I promise."

They took off, jogging first, and then speeding up as they found a pace that suited them both. Will flitted around them like a luminous hummingbird. It was hard to run in her bulky clothes, and harder still to tell how much progress they were making. Scales and mist blurred and blended together. Precious seconds bled away in streams.

There was no warning, nothing to prepare them before they reached the top. Ignis stopped so quickly she almost collided with him; they stood, panting, and took in their surroundings.

Here, the ridge on the dragon's back ended—or began— just below the slope of its skull. She couldn't make out details through the mist, but her eyes traced the shape of its furled ears, its long horns like daggers pointing back at them. A slow rushing sound filled the air, mingling with the whistle of the wind. The sound was coming from a place she couldn't see, on the other side of the dragon's head, where icy mist billowed out in plumes. Its breath, she realized.

The mist was lighter and patchier up here, and shifted more restlessly. Now that night had fallen, the world beyond was black, and she couldn't make out the train tracks or the shape of the ground. The ridge was too tall for her to look down the other side at Brume, but she could picture it: a modest cluster of homes and shops and just one school and one hospital, all peppered with electric lights.

She looked up instead, and her breath caught. This high above the lights of town, it was dark enough to see the stars. They were bright and glittering, too many to count, strewn across the canvas of the night sky. So much better and more brilliant than any picture or painting could ever capture.

"We made it," she said, laughing with relief.

"Roda."

Ignis's tone set alarm bells ringing in her head. He wasn't looking at her, or even at the sky. Instead, he stared ahead, fists clenched. Will hid, as if he'd sensed something wrong, too. But the only thing she saw was a bird perched on the end of the dragon's horn, pure white, so that it all but vanished into the mist.

No, she realized. Normal birds wove through gaps in the mist, never lingering long enough for its chill to stop their hearts; even a carrier pigeon equipped with the most potent warming enchantments money could buy wouldn't idle in a place like this. It wasn't a bird. It was an Aethon— an Aethon with white feathers.

The Traveler.

CH. 16

"HELLO?" RODA CALLED. "IS THAT YOU?"

The bird ruffled its feathers, fluttered off its perch, and transformed into the Traveler. He knelt between the dragon's horns. Through the mist, he was only an outline, a shadow with burning gold eyes.

Ignis flinched. "Don't—" he called out, but it was too late.

The Traveler pressed his palms flat against the dragon's scales and unleashed a shock of lightning. A powerful *crack* tore through the air as electricity poured from his splayed hands. It lit up his whole body white-gold— illuminating his gritted teeth, furrowed brow, and wild eyes for an instant—and lashed the dragon's slumbering features. A smell like burning filled Roda's nose, and the hair on her arms stood on end, but other than a staticky, stinging feeling, the Traveler's lightning didn't hurt her.

But Ignis's eyes were huge with fear. He took her gloved hand and placed it back on the ridge.

"Hold on," he told her. "Don't let go no matter what."

"What are you doing?" she shouted after him, but he was already racing up the dragon's neck, barreling toward the Traveler—trying to prevent his next strike.

He wasn't fast enough.

The Traveler shocked the dragon again, with another earsplitting *crack* and a brilliant, blinding flash of light. And again.

On the third strike, the dragon woke.

A shudder ran from its head down the coil of its back, where Roda stood. She clung to its spikes with both hands as the sudden movement almost sent her flying. But Ignis was still running, leaping atop the dragon's head to confront the Traveler—

The Traveler transformed, and so did Ignis. The two of them darted and wove through the air as crows, the black crow attacking while the white dodged easily.

The dragon shuddered again. Roda screamed as the world shook under her feet. Its head jerked, shaking off the pests flying around its snout. Ignis and the Traveler scattered.

The Traveler shot straight up and into the sky, swiftly vanishing from sight. Ignis tried to fly around to the dragon's back and land. But its head twisted to follow his flight path. She glimpsed the corner of one hazy, ice-encrusted silver eye, which was open only a sliver, as if the dragon was still half-asleep.

With a sound like wind rattling frost-covered tree branches, it exhaled a mighty gust of freezing mist. It engulfed Ignis completely and blew him off course. He spun in the air, tumbling beak over tail feathers, righted himself briefly, and half flew, half crashed onto the dragon's back.

The great, orb-like eye slid shut again, and its frozen scales stilled under her feet. Its head sank down into its shroud of mist once more. It was going back to sleep.

But Ignis wasn't moving.

His small form lay crumpled on the scales. Frost crept over him, turning black to white.

"No, no, no," Roda whispered, falling to her knees beside him. She picked him up, hands clumsy with the gloves, and tried to wipe the ice off him. But the material of her gloves and coat were freezing, too, and where her fingers brushed his feathers, more frost burst into existence, spreading outward in complex patterns, swirling delicately up and down the length of his wings.

She turned him over. His eyes were closed; ice had sealed his beak shut. Will hovered close by, flickering anxiously, his light reflecting off the frost and making it seem as though Ignis were coated in gold.

"What do I do?" she asked helplessly, as if expecting Will to have the answer. He didn't, but he dove at her collar and hovered there insistently until she looked down at him.

At the pocket watch around her neck. Which told her that she had one minute left before Kader's Comet would cross the sky. She had to be ready. But Ignis couldn't fly them up, not now, and if she didn't do something fast, he'd freeze to death.

He just needs to be warm, she thought. And she knew what she had to do.

She ripped off her hood, scarf, and goggles. The cold slammed into her. Shivering, she tucked Ignis into the hood and wrapped the scarf snugly over him. Then she got to her feet, clutching the bundle to her chest. It wasn't so different, she thought, from the day she'd first found him. Except this time, she wouldn't be jumping on her bike and riding home. She jogged up the dragon's neck and onto its crown, between its horns. Its brow ridges were dark hills near her feet. Her breath puffed into the air; she shook her hair out of her face so she wouldn't have to watch as the ends turned white. Soon it would be at the roots. The edges of her vision paled as her eyelashes, too, bleached in the cold.

Still no sign of the Traveler. If he came back, she had no way to defend herself.

Atop the dragon's head, she was level with the highest edges of the mist. Its upper layer dissipated into the air. Up here, the sky went on forever in every direction.

Then a light ignited at the farthest edge of the sky, like white fire.

Kader's Comet.

Ten seconds left.

Anonymous's note said to catch the comet. It didn't say *fly to* the comet. It said *catch.*

Nine seconds.

Roda thrust her hand up into the air, palm out. Ignis-the-crow rested in the crook of her elbow; she held him as tight as she dared.

Eight.

The comet burned through the sky, growing bigger, and

bigger, and bigger. It wasn't above her anymore. She was in its path. From this angle, it was so large it filled her entire field of vision, a flare of light sweeping toward her, and in the center of it all—darkness.

Seven.

The light grew so bright she had to shut her eyes. It *burned*. As it engulfed her completely, her feet left the ground and a violent wind buffeted her. Was she falling?

Six.

The wind pushed her body against something firm, and her hand dropped, scrabbling for purchase until it landed on a cool, metallic object. She opened her eyes and found herself balanced precariously on a stone step, holding on to the knob of a plain wooden door, the ground far, far away. She was *in* the comet. Or whatever it was. Because it *wasn't* a comet, not really. Comets didn't have doors.

Her feet almost slipped off the narrow step; only her grip on the doorknob kept her in place. Unable to hear anything above the wind or see anywhere else to go— with absolutely no other choice left—she turned the knob and fell through the open door.

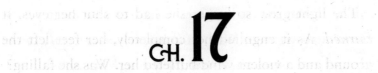

CH. 17

FIVE.

She couldn't catch herself without letting go of Ignis, so she hit the ground hard, slamming elbow-first into gleaming jade tiles. Pain shot up her arm. She groaned, flopping onto her back.

Lamplight washed the high stone ceiling orange-yellow. Gritting her teeth against the pain, she lifted her head and twisted around. The jade tiles stretched down a hallway so long she couldn't see the end of it. Beside her, the door she'd come in through swung wildly on its hinges as the wind whipped past its frame.

Next to it was another door. And another next to that one. And another . . .

Four.

The hallway was lined with so many doors she could not count them all, each about ten paces apart and identical.

There had only been one door on the outside. She was sure of it. But she remembered all too clearly what Anonymous had written: *What is a place you can only enter through one door, but can leave through many?*

Three.

All the doors were shut except for hers, and the one to its left, which opened onto the black night sky. The howl of the cold wind poured through its opening. Her eyes dropped to the floor, where lay a single white feather.

The Traveler had been here. He must have come through the same door as Roda. But there was no sign of him now. Had he left? Was he the one who'd opened the second door?

Two.

But then why hadn't Roda seen him come out?

Still clutching Ignis, afraid to set him down here, she sat up on her knees and reached for the feather.

One.

The door vanished. The roar of the wind ceased.

In the next instant, the feather was gone, too; the other

doors disappeared one by one, leaving nothing behind but bare stone walls.

There was a *pop*, and then a sound like someone riffling an oversized deck of cards. The hallway *shrank*. Its walls pulled in like an accordion being squeezed shut, the stones zipping past her in a blur and the tiles sliding under her feet. The ends of the hallway were visible, then, flying toward her from either side.

There was no escape.

They were going to crush her.

She screamed and curled up into a ball, holding Ignis much too tightly—

Then the riffling sound stopped. Her breath came in short, quick gasps, and her heart hammered like it meant to break out of her ribs and make a run for it. But she was, somehow, still alive.

When she lifted her head, the walls had stopped moving, and the place that had once been an endless hallway was now the size of a closet. An old-fashioned oil lamp hung on the wall. A new door had replaced the vanished ones; it was rough-hewn, with whorls like thumbprints punctuating the grain of the wood.

She checked on Ignis, lifting a flap of the cloth covering him. He was still unconscious, still coated in frost, which melted slowly into feathers that grew paler with every passing moment. His beak was white as marble.

Knees shaking, she pushed herself to her feet. Her free hand found the doorknob and twisted it open—

—and she stepped out into starlight.

She leaned against the doorframe, blinking in amazement. Before her was a space that might've once been an open-air courtyard: a broad, square expanse of flagstone enclosed by low walls. It was crumbling and yellowed, with spiderweb cracks marring the stone. A glass dome enclosed the courtyard and Roda within it. An indigo-black ocean vaulted over her head, glittering with stars. There was no other light source; the starshine was as bright as day.

A monument at least two stories tall stood in the middle of the courtyard. It depicted an old man whose noble features were weathered and creased with age—an aquiline nose over a full, neatly trimmed beard and moustache; a high forehead and hooded, deep-set eyes. He wore the elaborately embroidered robes of the bygone guildmages, open over a workman's tunic, breeches, boots, and gloves. His hands were clasped together at his rib cage, and draped over his shoulders was the unmistakable likeness of an ice dragon, its tail coiled around the plinth and its head resting near his chest, staring outward in eternal vigilance.

She didn't need to read the carved words on his pedestal to know the man's name; she'd only seen that face a million times in her schoolbooks. It was Aurelion Kader, the famous astronomer mage of centuries past. The one who'd built the bunker where the Traveler had imprisoned them, and the one responsible for enchanting the ice dragons.

Did this place belong to him, too?

Through the dome, spires and battlements stood stark against the dark sky. Her eyes traced a staircase that wound over an outer wall, unprotected from the void of space. She could even make out the chipped shingles on the sloped roof of the nearest tower, and the reflection of stars on the windowpanes.

She was in a castle, and also somehow still inside the comet, traveling through outer space. It was impossible, but the way her muscles ached from the climb and her stomach panged with hunger were too real to be a dream.

Will bounced into view inches from her face, almost blinding her.

"You made it!" she said, relieved. He must've hitched a ride on her collar, and the wind had failed to shake him off.

"*Need warm*," he wheezed.

Right. The bundle of feathers and cloth in her arms felt heavier and heavier the longer she stood there. She turned to close the door behind her, but . . . there *was* no door. Nothing but a solid wall in the spot where she had just come in. She swallowed hard, unnerved. But there was no time to worry about disappearing hallways. She set off at a brisk stride, following the perimeter of the courtyard until she reached another door.

It was locked. She kept going.

The next door opened onto an unlit stairwell. She balked at the yawning blackness awaiting her below. Even with her flashlight, she didn't really want to go down there. Not unless it was her only option.

The third door revealed another set of stairs, but this one was warm and lantern-lit. The familiar crackling song of a fire echoed out from it.

If there was a fire, then there had to be someone tending it. Anonymous?

Open the door. I'll be waiting for you.

Her stomach squirmed the way it did before a big test at school.

She took a first, shaky step down. When nothing happened—no chasms opening under her feet, no ghouls springing out of the shadows—she threw caution to the wind and took the remaining steps as fast as she could without jostling Ignis too much.

Please be all right, she thought, rounding a bend in the staircase. *After all this, you'd better be all right.*

CH. 18

SHE STUMBLED OUT INTO A LARGE ROOM BRIMMING WITH firelight, and so warm she instantly began to sweat under her many layers. Rows of countertops and cabinets divided the space into corridors. Past their gleaming silver surfaces, flames roared in a fireplace taller than Roda herself.

But she'd been wrong. No one else was here.

No one she could see, anyway. The empty kitchen was nevertheless full of movement. In the nearest corner, a knife chopped away at a mound of plump brown mushrooms, rising and falling over the cutting board as if held by an invisible hand. A wooden spoon stirred a pot of stew in jerky, rhythmic motions, left-right-up-down-left-right. Two sacks of rice scooted past her, hopped into the air, and deposited themselves on a counter.

Will floated to the knife, hovering over its handle curiously. The *clack-clack-clack* of the blade on the cutting board did not so much as slow.

The Roda of two days ago would've been petrified. But it was hard to be intimidated by silverware after she'd met a dragon.

She adjusted her grip on Ignis and made her way through the kitchen, dodging a broom that beat rather aggressively at the floor, until she reached the fireplace. A half circle of firelight clasped the hearth like an apron. That was where she set Ignis down, as close to the fire as she dared.

She peeled off her layers until she was left in the pants, T-shirt, and jacket she'd worn to school the day before. Unwrapping Ignis from his cold, wet coverings, she transferred him to a lumpy nest she'd made using the driest pieces of her discarded clothing. The fire would warm him up quickly. She hoped.

Once Ignis was settled in, her neglected stomach unleashed a growl that would've made a bear envious. She was *starving*. The sounds of chopping and sizzling carried over to her on rosemary-scented air.

There was plenty of food. It couldn't hurt to take a little bit.

Who are they cooking for? she wondered. *How many people are there in this place?*

The invisible cooks didn't stop her as she grabbed two wooden bowls out of a cabinet. These, thankfully, didn't seem inclined to move on their own. Warily, she approached the tub-sized pot simmering on one of the three stoves. A ladle stirred lazy circles through the thick stew within. When her fingers touched its handle, it stilled and fell into her hand. She spooned out two generous servings of stew for herself and Ignis. It was golden, spiced, and filled with tender pieces of meat and vegetables. When she released the ladle, it went on stirring as if nothing had happened.

She helped herself to two thick slices of warm bread that a serrated knife was carving from a loaf. It was fluffy white inside, with a crisp brown crust that made a satisfying *crack* each time the blade cut into it. An inspection of some nearby drawers produced spoons. Victorious, she returned to Ignis with her spoils.

He hadn't woken yet. She set his food on the ground nearby, where the fire would keep it warm, and dug into hers. She was too hungry to care what it tasted like—she'd have eaten just about anything—but it was *amazing*. Even the vegetables were good, and the broth warmed her from the inside out. The bread soaked it up and practically dissolved on her tongue. She shoveled heaping spoonfuls into her mouth until there was only broth left, which she slurped up until the bowl was spotless. Resisting the urge to go back for seconds, she set the bowl aside and wiped her mouth on her sleeve.

Ignis hadn't moved at all. The ice had melted away, and Roda winced at the sight of his feathers: they had gone pure white, not a drop of black left.

"We match," she said, tucking a lock of her own white hair behind her ear. She nudged him very gently. "Come on. Wake up. We're *here*! We made it!"

She pulled his bowl closer and carefully spooned out a few drops of broth.

"I brought you food," she said. "Go on and eat."

His eyes opened a crack. Weakly, he lifted his head and dipped his beak into the spoonful of broth. When it was gone, she spooned up some more, which he drank as well. When she lowered the spoon a third time, Ignis was getting to his feet, wings dragging on the floor. He surveyed their surroundings for a second, then her, and at last shifted back into his human form.

He was dry but bedraggled, and his white hair was a shocking contrast to his ash-gray skin. His eyes dropped to the bowl Roda held out to him, to the pile of clothes he'd been sleeping in, and finally to Will. The wisp bounced happily in place, as if pleased Ignis was all right.

He turned to her. "What in the world—"

Uh-oh.

He'd seen Roda's white hair, and it was clear by the look on his face that he'd guessed what that meant for him.

"Ignis," she said, in the tones one might use to placate a disturbed horse. "It's just hair. It's all right."

"*No*," he whispered. He looked back at the nest, reached down, and picked a dove-white feather out of its folds. His other hand flew to his hair, pulling at it helplessly. He plucked out a strand and whimpered when he saw it. "I look like an old man!"

"Aren't you hungry?" she said, trying to distract him. "Eat. It's good."

"If I ever see that charlatan again, I'm going to *kill* him."

She sighed. "I don't think you will. The Traveler's gone."

"Gone?"

He picked up his bowl, stirring its contents sullenly. Once he took the first bite, though, he set upon the meal as eagerly as Roda had. She filled him in on what had happened while he'd been unconscious. Will drifted away to explore.

"So we're in a *space castle*," he said. "Did you see any shops on your way down here? Or forests to hunt in, or farms to grow wheat? Where did all this come from? It doesn't make sense!"

"Maybe it's magic," she said.

"Even magic makes sense. It has rules."

"But we don't know what the rules are. That's why it doesn't make sense to us." She stood up and surveyed the countertops, the ingredients laid out in various stages of preparation, the wooden handles of the utensils waving merrily as they worked. "But maybe we can figure it out."

Along one wall was a row of sliding doors. She tugged one aside to reveal a pantry. Its compartments were piled high with every variety of bread imaginable: rolls and loaves she could've found in her own neighborhood bakery; heaps of the thin, flat rounds favored in Uskana; hard crusts with a fine layer of powdery flour and pillowy soft buns with golden crowns; breads embedded with pieces of fruit, with grains and nuts, with swirls of cinnamon.

She spotted one of the oversized loaves of fluffy white bread she'd eaten earlier. Experimentally, she pulled it off the shelf, hoping to see a label on its paper wrapping that might hint at where it had come from.

But as soon as she did, a new one appeared out of thin air to take its place.

She gasped. "Did you see that?"

"That doesn't answer any of our questions," Ignis

complained. "That makes things *worse*."

She shoved the loaf back onto the shelf and returned to the fireplace. "I think kitchen magic is the least of our concerns right now."

They dumped Anonymous's letters out on the floor while Will inspected a pile of junk in the opposite corner. Bending their heads together, they pored over each of the notes, lingering on every word and speculating about hidden patterns and clues.

"'I'll be waiting for you,'" Ignis read. "We're here, and Anonymous isn't. Even though we did everything we were supposed to do! So what now?"

But Roda felt certain Anonymous *was* here. Somewhere.

"Look at this one again. It makes sense now. *Leave in ten seconds or stay for ten years.*" That was the line that bothered her the most. "It took ten seconds for Kader's Comet to cross the sky, and when the ten seconds were over, all the doors disappeared."

"So we can only get into this place, *or* get out, when Kader's Comet appears," Ignis said, following her logic.

"Which is every ten years, for three nights in a row. Tomorrow is day three. So if we don't find Anonymous and leave tomorrow before that ten-second window ends—"

"Then we're stuck here," he finished.

If that happened, Mom would never wake up, and Ignis would never have the answers he'd been hoping for.

They traded nervous glances.

But before anything else could be said, a loud *clack* made them jump. From a darkened corner on the far side of the fireplace, two blazing yellow lights came on.

What Roda had mistaken for a rubbish heap was an automaton.

It was humanoid, with two arms ending in five-fingered hands, two legs, a dented and scorched metallic torso, and a hinged jaw that opened and shut—that was the source of the clacking noise. Joints creaking, the automaton unfolded itself from the corner until it stood at its full height and beamed its electric eyes in their direction.

Roda and Ignis leapt to their feet.

"We didn't mean to intrude," Roda said, holding up her hands palms-out.

"Stay back!" Ignis's fists were clenched, lightning playing over his knuckles.

The automaton took a jerky step toward them.

"*Rrr*," it growled. It coughed out smoke and tried again. With a voice like static electricity, it said: "*Rooooh-da.*"

Her mouth fell open. "Will?"

CH. 19

SHE HELPED THE AUTOMATON MOVE TO THE FIREPLACE, his knobby metal fingers on her shoulder, his tin body leaning on hers as he figured out how to walk. Ignis kept his distance as Will sat down clumsily, dropping to the floor with a raucous clatter like pots and pans banging together. She sank down beside him, and he immediately mimicked her posture, curling up with his arms around his knees.

Up close, she had a better view of the damage to his frame. Panels were missing from his torso, so that she could see the wires and bolts within. Dents and scuffs marred his limbs, and his jaw was skewed, as if it had been torn off and then shoved carelessly back into place.

"How did you get in there?" she asked. "Are you stuck?"

"*I . . . like it here,*" Will said in his new mechanical voice, his crooked jaw working. "*Like having hands. Like having . . . memories.*"

"Memories?" Ignis said. His distrustful frown faded, and he knelt on Will's other side. "What do you remember?"

"*Someone,*" he said, "*made me.*"

The way Will spoke as if he was *becoming* the automaton worried her.

"Are you sure you don't want to come out of there, Will?" she asked. "What if you get stuck?"

"*Sure,*" Will said firmly.

It sort of made sense. The wisps were Aurelion Kader's assistants, created specifically to help him with his work. Maybe that included his experiments and inventions. If that was the case, then an affinity for technology was in Will's nature.

"Who made you?" Ignis pressed.

"*Lives here. Alone. Built me for . . .*"

"For what?"

"*Company,*" Will said after a pause, as if he'd struggled to recall the right word. "*But I was not enough. I was only a machine.*"

Not anymore, she thought.

"*My creator learned from the notes left behind by a mage who died many years ago,*" Will said, speaking more quickly and confidently with every passing second. "*But he could not master invention. He turned to other arts instead and abandoned me.*"

"Did he do *that* to you?" Roda demanded, gesturing at his injuries.

"Yes," Will said. "*My creator was ill-tempered. Impatient. Restless from years of isolation. Sometimes, he lashed out. He always fixed me later. Then he stopped.*"

"Is he—is he still here?" she asked. "How long ago did this happen?"

Will's dented skull tilted thoughtfully, as if studying an internal clock that had never stopped ticking. "*Four years, six months, and three days ago.*"

"Then he *could* still be here. Unless he left last night."

"Someone has to be eating this food," Ignis said, sweeping his hand toward the bustling kitchen. "He's definitely still here. A prince in an empty castle." He shook his head. "No wonder he's unhinged."

"*He wears no crown, and this place is no castle.*"

"Fine," Ignis said, "but I'm not calling him *creator*."

"If it's not a castle, then what is it?" Roda asked.

"It is Nowhere."

She and Ignis traded glances. Their theories had been right: Nowhere was a place, and Anonymous had been preparing Roda to make the journey here from their very first letter.

But why? she thought. *Why do all this? Why poison Mom just to get me here?*

A new, alarming idea occurred to her then. "What if the Prince is Anonymous?"

"But how could he have delivered the letters?" Ignis pointed out. "If we're right, then he's been stuck here for the last ten years."

"Will," she said. "If the Prince was still around, where would we find him?"

If they could find out more about the Prince, maybe they could learn more about Nowhere, too, and figure out what Anonymous wanted from them.

Joints whining with every move, Will clambered to his feet.

"The library," he said. *"He would be in the library."*

They wound their way through Nowhere's halls, treading over intricately patterned rugs and past paintings of long-dead lords and ladies. But the paints and dyes had faded with time, and many of the passageways were unlit. It was like walking through a blurry memory.

Still, the place was spotless, every inch of it. They passed a hallway where a mop danced up and down the tiles; around the corner, a polishing cloth scrubbed at a carved silver frame. Just as the kitchen was equipped with cooking spells, the rest of Nowhere apparently had cleaning spells to keep it tidy.

Each window they passed offered a glimpse of the castle's outer walls, startlingly pale against the starry depths of space.

"*We're here*," Will said, coming to an abrupt stop before a pair of oaken double doors. The frame was embellished with carvings of ice dragons. Their slender bodies twisted and twined over one another, snakelike, and every scale had been rendered in meticulous detail. Even the doorknobs had been sculpted in the shape of talons.

Roda hesitated. "So the Prince might be in there right now?"

"*Perhaps.*"

"What do we even say to him?" she asked Ignis.

"We'll demand answers. If he wants us to leave, all he has to do is tell us what we need to know." He bared his sharp teeth in a fearless grin. "Ready?"

The apprehension she expected to feel wasn't there. They had faced worse than this mysterious Prince. She nodded, and they turned in unison to face the double doors. Roda took a deep breath, preparing herself for what she might find inside.

Someone who built things and then destroyed them on a whim.

Someone who had been alone in Nowhere for at least ten years.

Someone angry.

Steeling herself, she reached for the shining bronze handle and pushed the door open.

The library was twice the size of the courtyard, and it, too, had a transparent ceiling. Rows of bookcases stretched away over a jade-tiled floor, illuminated only by the starlight from above and the handful of oil lanterns set into the stone walls. It was elegant, shadowed, and lovely.

And it was a mess.

Books had been pulled off the shelves and never replaced, instead left in piles on the ground, some of which were as tall as a grown man. Here and there, empty mugs and glasses littered the shelves. A brush and dustpan worked diligently in one corner, sweeping the floor, but cobwebs clung to the sconces and a faint musty smell permeated the whole room.

It needed a couple of open windows. It needed someone with eyes to do the cleaning. Above all else, it desperately needed a librarian.

"No one's even here," Ignis said, disappointed.

Roda felt a little deflated, too, after mentally preparing herself to meet the Prince. To maybe meet Anonymous, at last, and get the answers that would bring her that smallest bit closer to saving Mom. Instead what they'd found was a dead end. Frustration mounted in her chest.

"Will?" she said, suppressing the urge to scream. "Is there anywhere else he could be?"

But Will was wandering away down the stacks, his metal feet clanging on the tiles.

"Where are you going?" she called.

He didn't respond. Roda followed him, Ignis trailing along after her.

A desk was tucked away in the far corner of the library. A lantern hung over its surface, which overflowed with handwritten journals and open books.

"My creator did most of his research here," Will said.

Gingerly, Roda picked up one of the journals. The paper was yellowed with age, the ink faded in places. Some of the pages contained sketches and diagrams. Many others were covered with cramped writing she found difficult to read, the letters joined and all running together in tangles. It reminded her of the ones the Traveler had sifted through back in the bunker.

The front cover fell open in her hands, and sure enough, the author had signed his name on the first page: Aurelion Kader.

"Ignis, look," she said, turning the journal so he could read the name. "It's more of Kader's work."

"That would explain this." Ignis held up the one he'd been examining. "These are enchantments—you can tell because they're in mage-script."

Roda leaned closer, but the lines swam through her vision. "I can't read it. The letters keep moving and bumping into each other."

"They're protected by some kind of spell. I guess it doesn't work on Aethons." He shrugged and kept flipping through the book. "Doesn't matter, because I don't know enough mage-script to read it, either. It's a completely different language."

Roda shut the journal with a snap and surveyed the cluttered desktop.

"Kader's been dead for a long time," she said. "Now

the Prince is here, going through his research. What's he looking for?"

"*I don't know,*" Will said. "*His ramblings always confused me.*"

"I can't tell, either, not at a glance," Ignis said with a frustrated shake of his head. "If we just had a little more time to look through all this . . ."

"We have to find Anonymous," she said. "Let's get out of here."

He nodded and dropped the book on the table carelessly.

It fell open to a new page, and something on it made him do a double take.

"Ignis?"

"Wait," he murmured, bending over the book again.

She peeked over his shoulder. Spread across two pages was a diagram composed of arrows and curves, some cutting straight across the page and some splitting into branches. Beside them, in the familiar cramped writing that filled all the other texts, were notes written in mage-script. The letters didn't move this time—there was no protective enchantment on it—and while she couldn't understand what it said, she noticed that spellwords and equations flowed uninterrupted into one another, as if Kader had merged magic and mathematics.

"Are you seeing this?" Ignis asked.

"It looks like a mess to me."

"It's not! It's genius!" he said. "Kader was working on *time travel*."

"That's what the Prince has been researching?" she asked, uneasy.

"Maybe. I wish I understood what this said," Ignis muttered, squinting down at the diagram. He pulled the other journals closer, flipping through them with purpose this time. Over and over, he found variations on the same image, as well as journal entries peppered with bits of equation-spells that matched the ones in the diagrams.

There was an enthralled gleam in Ignis's eyes, like he couldn't have looked away if he'd tried. Roda wanted to rip the journals out of his hands.

"Ignis," she hissed. "We have to go."

"Don't you understand? If time travel is *real*, if it's possible, then imagine what you could do with it!"

"All I want to do is go home. And we can't do that until we find Anonymous."

"'We'?" Ignis said. When he lifted his head, his face

was scarily blank. "*You* can go home. *You* can see your mother again. I can't. Not ever. Unless—"

A noise startled Ignis into silence. It was the unmistakable sound of a door creaking open.

CH. 20

THE POUNDING OF BOOTS ON TILE ECHOED THROUGH THE
library. They had no time to react; the stranger was almost
upon them—

A white-haired figure burst out from behind the nearest
bookcase, long skirt swirling around her legs. Her blue
eyes were wide, her chest heaving with every breath. When
she caught sight of them, the corners of her lips twitched
up in what might have been a triumphant smile.

It was Aunt Dora.

"What—" Roda began, but Aunt Dora crossed the
space between them in a few quick strides and took her
by the shoulders.

"It's not safe here," she said, her eyes darting between

Roda and Ignis. "You need to hide."

Aunt Dora gave Roda a gentle push toward the far side of the library, where the aisles were cloaked in shadow. Roda clutched at Aunt Dora's sleeve, not willing to leave her side yet. They'd *just* found each other, and all Roda wanted was to hear her say that everything would be all right. That Mom was going to be fine. That she would fix it, the way Aunt Dora always fixed everything.

"He's coming," she said. "There's no time. *Hide!*"

"You can't just—" Roda protested. But Ignis took Aunt Dora's warning seriously. He grabbed Roda's hand and pulled her after him to the back row. Roda hooked her arm around Will's. The three of them dove behind the shelves and crouched low—just in time. The library doors flew open again with such force, they slammed against the walls.

Footsteps struck the tiles, fast and urgent. Roda and Ignis pushed aside some of the books to make a window in the shelf, through which they could see Aunt Dora leaning over the desk. Reverently, she plucked one of the journals from the haphazard pile and paged through it.

A figure loomed out of the darkness.

Tall and thin and cloaked in black, his presence alone made the starlight dimmer. His clenched fists and stiff shoulders radiated anger. The ends of his mist-bleached white hair curled over the back of his neck and disappeared into his high collar. From her angle, Roda couldn't see his face; she fought the instinct to shrink away and tried to memorize every detail about him she could. This had to be the Prince of Nowhere.

"How did you even learn to read this?" Aunt Dora asked. She waved the journal carelessly.

"Put that *down*."

That voice was somehow familiar.

"Why should I? It's not yours. All of this belongs to Professor Kader."

A beat of irritated silence passed.

"Is this where you've been hiding all day?"

All day? That meant Aunt Dora had gotten here last night, when Roda was watching the comet pass by with her classmates. She must've left in the morning to make the journey in time. At least that explained why she hadn't been around when Anonymous had attacked Mom.

"Oh, here and there," Aunt Dora said. She turned a page. "So. Ten years, huh? Was it worth it?"

"It's going to be," he said.

Aunt Dora closed the book and set it down gently on the desk. "You don't have to do this."

"You don't understand. You never did." He stepped closer, towering over her by several inches, but she didn't appear the slightest bit cowed.

Roda couldn't stand to watch him loom over Aunt Dora like that. It made her heart clench with fear. She looked down, swallowing hard, her gaze landing instead on the bookshelf inches away from her nose. The titles nearest to her read: *Advanced Mystical Mechanics*; *The Definitive Guide to Thaumaturgical Engineering*; *Neurosorcery, Third Edition* . . . She didn't fully register the words or what they meant until she reached the next one, which snagged at her attention, catching on her thoughts like a burr. It was a thin tome that had passed through many hands, judging from the way its spine was scuffed and cracked. The binding was loose, so that some of the pages stuck out at the corners; it was so old it was falling apart. She had to read its faded title three times before she could believe what she was seeing.

"You've already gotten in my way twice," the Prince was saying, though Roda's heartbeat was so loud she barely heard him. "Tonight is my last chance, and I'm not letting you ruin it."

Impulsively, Roda slid the book off the shelf, ignoring the perplexed look Ignis shot her, and stuffed it into her backpack. She forced herself to concentrate on Aunt Dora and the Prince again.

"Letting me?" Aunt Dora said, raising one pale eyebrow. "When did I ask for your permission?"

His gloved hand lifted, as if to touch Aunt Dora's cheek, but instead, he tugged at the cord of the necklace she wore, pulling until the ring popped out from her collar.

"*Don't*," she snarled, batting his hand away.

"You still wear that trinket? How . . . sweet," he said mockingly.

An awful suspicion stirred in Roda's mind then.

"I bet you still have yours," Aunt Dora said.

No, she thought. *It can't be.*

Because there was only one person she knew who had a ring that matched Aunt Dora's.

"Believe what you want," he said. "But we're not staying here. Are you going to follow me, or will I have to make you?"

"Depends," Aunt Dora said. "How do you plan on making me do anything?"

"I won't. But *they* will."

A *whoosh* of air and a beating sound heralded the arrival of something huge and winged. Two—three somethings, soaring through the library. Roda couldn't see them from where she knelt, but their immense shapes blocked out the starlight and made the shadows ripple.

They alighted atop the bookcases, well out of Roda's line of sight. Aunt Dora leaned back as if to get a better look.

"Nowhere has its defenses," the Prince said. "I decided to make some of my own."

Roda held her breath, mentally pleading for him to turn. She had to see him and find out for sure if she was right, but she couldn't be right; it was impossible—

"I'm outnumbered." Aunt Dora laid a hand on the desk and gazed down at the heaps of research with something like longing. "You win. For now."

She walked past him, chin up, as if she was the one in charge here. He turned to follow, and that was when Roda saw his face.

Beside her, Ignis gasped, but Aunt Dora coughed into her sleeve at the same moment, so it went unheard. The man escorting her from the library wasn't human; he was an Aethon, with the same distinctive ash-gray skin and golden eyes as Ignis.

It was the Traveler.

But *older*.

Roda's stomach lurched, as if she were falling from a

great height. In the hour or two since she'd last seen the Traveler, he had somehow aged *years*. But that wasn't possible.

Unless Professor Kader hadn't just been researching time travel. He'd figured it out, and Nowhere was the key.

The Traveler—no, the *Prince* marched Aunt Dora out of the library. The flying creatures followed, soaring over the shelves and out into the hall. The doors closed behind them.

"Will? Was that man your creator?" she asked faintly.

Will had kept perfectly still while they'd eavesdropped. He crouched next to them, knobby hands clinging to the edge of the shelf, and only relaxed when Roda broke her silence. His neck creaked noisily as he rotated his head to face her.

"*Yes*," he said. And then, more quietly, with a whir to his voice: "*Don't like him*."

She jumped to her feet. "We have to follow them."

Ignis was slower to rise. One look at him made her discard whatever it was she'd been about to say next.

"What's wrong?" she asked instead.

His skin had gained a green tinge, and his hands shook. "That man—"

"—was the Traveler," Roda finished.

He blinked at her. "What?"

She hurriedly explained about the rings, his voice, his appearance—all the reasons she was certain the Prince and the Traveler were one and the same.

"But it doesn't make sense," Ignis said in barely more than a whisper. "How could . . . why . . ."

"We need to talk to Aunt Dora," she said. "She must know what's going on. Maybe she even knows what happened to Anonymous."

His expression closed off.

"You're right," he said. "Let's go talk to . . . to Aunt Dora."

They crept out of the library and snuck down the halls, Will tiptoeing behind them, following the fast-fading sound of beating wings.

CH. 21

THE PRINCE TOOK AUNT DORA TO THE OUTER REACHES of the castle, where it was dusty and abandoned.

Will hung back, trying not to creak, while Roda and Ignis peeked around the corner. The Prince threw open a door and stood back until Aunt Dora vanished inside. His winged guards were gone now.

"You realize that if you lock me in," Aunt Dora said, "I'll miss my chance to leave tonight. I'll be trapped here. We both will be."

"We won't be trapped," he said dismissively. "I'll have mastered Nowhere's powers. I'll be able to take us wherever, *whenever* we want."

"And if you fail?"

"I won't." He leaned against the doorframe, arms folded. Roda couldn't see his expression. Her ears strained to catch his next words. "I know the children are here."

Beside her, Ignis flinched. Roda held her breath; her sweaty palms slipped on the stone wall.

The Prince was still speaking. "You remember it all, don't you? I don't know how. I don't know why the leaving enchantment didn't work on you. But you remember."

There was a long silence. Then, almost too quietly for Roda to hear, Aunt Dora said: "You're not going to save anyone this way."

"If you know where they are, just tell me," he snapped.

"I don't."

One of them sighed. There was no telling which.

"They were climbing the mist all day. They would've been hungry, tired. The boy was unconscious and freezing," the Prince said, thinking aloud. "And the girl would have . . . she would've wanted to help him. She would have wanted to take him someplace warm."

"Yes. She would have," Aunt Dora said. Her tone carried layers of meaning Roda had no clue how to translate. Why was Aunt Dora speaking so calmly to someone who was treating her like a prisoner?

"They went to the kitchen, didn't they?"

"I suppose."

The Prince stepped out of the doorway.

"I'm right. Do you know how I know?" His lips twisted in a painful-looking smile. "After all these years, I'm different. But you . . . you're almost exactly the same." He grabbed the doorknob and shot her a final, parting glare. "Do *not* mess this up for me."

"I live to spoil your fun."

He snorted. "Truer words."

The door shut with a decisive *click*. The Prince rested his fingers on the doorknob, bowed his head, and muttered a few words Roda couldn't understand. Then he swept away down the hall and swiftly vanished.

Minutes passed. Only when she was certain that the Prince would not return did Roda run to the door and rattle the knob.

"Aunt Dora?" she said, her mouth almost pressed against the wood. There was no answer.

A hysterical laugh bubbled up in her chest; she clamped her lips together to keep it inside. Only a thin door separated Roda from the one person in the world she most wanted to see right now, other than Mom. The person she'd thought of every time she'd needed to be brave. The person who might finally be able to give her some answers.

Just one door, and it stopped her as effectively as another dragon.

"Let me try," Ignis said, pale and subdued. His bravado from before they'd entered the library was gone. Roda didn't blame him. Their situation was more dire than she'd ever thought. The Prince was *hunting* them.

She moved over so Ignis could take her place. His fingers had barely brushed the doorknob before a soft *click* signaled the lock opening.

"How did you—" Roda asked.

"He—he must have made it so that only an Aethon could open it," Ignis said, not looking at her.

The chamber within contained a cot, but no other furnishings. Her aunt stood beside the leaded window, hands resting on the edge, gazing through the distortion of its diamond panes at the scattered stars outside. Calm as anything. It almost felt like they were disturbing her.

"You're here," she said, turning, a relieved smile breaking out over her face.

Will's footsteps clanked over the tiles, following them into the room; Ignis shut the door. But Roda couldn't tear her eyes away from Aunt Dora's smile.

Why wasn't Aunt Dora surprised to see her? In the library, too. She'd been expecting them.

Roda could no longer ignore the awful suspicion spreading like an infection under the surface of her mind. The truth had been in front of her all along. She just hadn't wanted to believe it.

"Aunt Dora," she said. "You're the one who sent me those letters, aren't you? You're Anonymous."

Please tell me I'm wrong.

"Yes," Aunt Dora said, without any sign of regret. "I am."

CH. 22

HER MIND BLANKED OUT. ALL SHE WANTED WAS TO WIPE that infuriatingly calm expression off Aunt Dora's face. She'd never hit anyone in her life, but she wanted to hit her now. She wanted to take her by the collar and shake her until she explained how she could have played such a sick game with her own niece, how she could have toyed with Mom's life, how she could have betrayed her only living family in such an unimaginable way.

She lunged, but Ignis caught her by the elbow before she could get very far.

"I know you're mad," Aunt Dora started.

"You lied to me!" Roda howled. She shook Ignis off. He'd slowed her down enough that her instant of blind fury had passed, but her body still trembled with suppressed rage. "You *hurt Mom*—"

"I had to get you here," Aunt Dora said. "I know what works on you and what doesn't."

No apology. No shame. Nothing could have fixed this, but Aunt Dora didn't even *try* to fix it. Ignis inched closer, silently offering support without trying to touch her again, but Roda felt far away from him, from this unfathomable moment, from everything.

To think that Roda had expected her aunt to *save them*. To think that Roda had blamed the notes on everyone else—Mr. Worrel, Ignis, the Traveler—except the most obvious suspect. She'd been the biggest fool, the easiest target. It had taken Aunt Dora no effort at all to trick her, because Roda had always believed every word she said. Believed in her stories and believed in *her*.

"*Why?*" Roda asked. The word cut her throat, as if it had barbs. She swallowed and tried again: "Why did you do it? And Mom—"

"Is completely fine. We can talk about her later. Right now—"

"*Later?* After everything— After what you put me through, you won't even—"

"Roda, wait," Ignis said. Betrayed, she turned to him,

but the look on his face was so bleak it dampened her rage. "When the Prince figures out we're not in the kitchen, he's going to come back here. We don't have much time."

Over his shoulder, her eyes found Will. He sat beside the door with his back to the wall, the battered struts making up his arms wrapped clumsily around his scuffed knees. His bulging yellow eyes gave him the permanently watchful expression of an owl, but more than that, he was still frightened from seeing the Prince. And Roda wasn't helping. Guiltily, she looked away.

Completely fine, Aunt Dora had said. Was that really true? Mom wasn't in danger after all? Even if Roda let herself believe it, she was too confused to feel any relief.

"You brought us here to stop him, didn't you?" Ignis said.

Aunt Dora sat down on the floor and gestured for them to follow. Ignis did. Roda, stubbornly, stayed standing, watching in silent fury as Aunt Dora took out the pen she kept in her boot.

"I need paper," she said. "Roda, may I have your letters back?"

Roda threw her backpack at Aunt Dora's head. She caught it.

"Right," Aunt Dora said, fishing out one of the notes.

She flipped it over to the blank side. "What have you managed to learn about this place so far?"

"Nothing," Ignis said. "Except that it has something to do with Aurelion Kader."

"Yes. Professor Kader called it Nowhere, because it exists outside of reality as we know it. It's not really *anywhere*, except for once every ten years, on three nights, for ten seconds each, when Nowhere touches our world. We can see its plane of existence brush against ours, disguised as the celestial object we know as Kader's Comet. And that is the only time you can get in *or* out of it."

Aunt Dora drew a double-sided arrow with a dash in the center splitting it in half.

"Nowhere was Professor Kader's great experiment with time travel, though it doesn't actually do the traveling itself," she said. "You enter through an endless corridor lined with doors. Right?"

Reluctantly, Roda nodded. *Mom is completely fine.* If it was true, then . . . she could afford to listen to Aunt Dora's explanation. Maybe then she'd understand what had compelled Aunt Dora to do something so drastic. Maybe it would feel like less of a betrayal.

"This dash in the middle," Aunt Dora said, tapping it with the end of her pen, "represents the door *you* came in through. But then, you must be wondering about all the other doors."

Even Will had scooted closer, listening intently. Aunt Dora drew more dashes on either side of the first, evenly spaced apart, and between each pair she wrote the number ten.

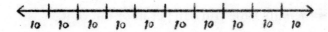

"All those doors are the *same* door," she said, "only they lead to different time periods. Each door is separated by ten years."

"'You can only enter through one door, but can leave through many,'" Roda said, recalling the line from Anonymous's note.

"Exactly. You enter Nowhere from your own time: only one door is accessible to you from the outside." Aunt Dora circled the middle dash. "You then have ten seconds to leave. You can exit through the same door you entered. Or you could go, say, three doors to the left"—she circled the corresponding dash, three marks down the line from the middle one—"and end up thirty years in the past."

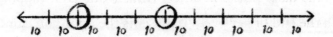

"Then could you go to the future, too?" Ignis asked.

"Yes."

"And if you went out the door to thirty years in the past," Roda said, thinking of the Traveler, "but then used the same door to come back *in*, you'd end up in Nowhere again. But not the same Nowhere you left. The Nowhere of thirty years ago."

She knelt, taking the pen from Aunt Dora and adding a mark of her own to the diagram.

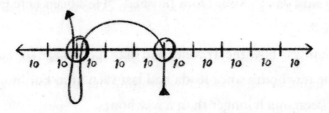

"You're getting it," Aunt Dora said approvingly. "The Prince has visited Nowhere three times and traveled to the past twice. He found this place as a child, and slowly the knowledge of its existence consumed him. He returned as a young man in his twenties, and went back in time twenty years, intending to change his past." Aunt Dora's voice faltered, and an expression of genuine pain crossed her face. "He failed."

"So he tried again," Ignis guessed.

"Yes. By the time Kader's Comet returned, he was over thirty years old and still determined to rewrite history. He made the trip to Nowhere one last time."

"That's when we met him as the Traveler," Roda said.

"Who?" Aunt Dora asked.

Grudgingly, Roda described their brief encounters with the Traveler. Aunt Dora seemed thrown for an instant, but she quickly rallied.

"Yes. When he entered Nowhere again, he went back in time ten years. From there, he reentered the Nowhere of ten years past," Aunt Dora finished. "He's been here ever since."

That was how the Traveler had managed to age so much in the few hours since Roda had last seen him. For him, it had been much longer than a few hours.

"*By accident?*" Will asked.

"No," Aunt Dora said. "He meant to stay. He wanted to study Nowhere from the inside."

Will tilted his head, puzzled. "*But he doesn't like it here.*"

"Yes. I know. He thought it a sacrifice worth making."

"Why bother going back at all if he was just going to stay inside Nowhere?" Roda asked. "He could've gone forward, or . . ."

"I don't think it ever occurred to him not to live in the past," Aunt Dora said coldly.

"Are you sure he didn't go back for *you*?"

It was a guess. A stab in the dark. Maybe the Traveler had only gone one door down because he'd known he didn't have much time to choose, and he had to give himself a few seconds to fly back *in*, too. But that choice had also guaranteed that he would wind up back in the present, where Aunt Dora was. Aunt Dora talked as if the Prince were an enemy and nothing more, but it was clear—from the rings, from the familiarity in the way they spoke to each other, from the suppressed emotion in Aunt Dora's voice now—that things weren't that simple.

Sure enough, Aunt Dora flinched as though she'd been struck. But she didn't respond. For once, she had no stories, no answers, nothing at all to say.

Ignis's head was bowed, eyes fixed on the drawing.

"He failed to change the past," Ignis said. "And now . . . ?"

"Now, he's trying again," Aunt Dora said, avoiding Roda's eyes. "But he doesn't want to follow Nowhere's

rules. He doesn't want to be limited to ten-year incre-
ments. He doesn't want to relive a whole decade, only to
fail. He's over forty years old now; a couple more failures,
and he'll be too old to try again."

"He wants unlimited do-overs," Ignis said. "If he fails,
he wants to be able to go back one day instead of ten years.
He'll relive the same day a thousand times if that's what
it takes." He blinked as if shaking himself out of a trance.
"Um. That's what I'm guessing, anyway. Right?"

"Right," Aunt Dora said. "He wants total control over
the timeline. He wants absolute freedom to travel forward
and back at will."

"That has nothing to do with me and Ignis," Roda
argued. "*You* stop the Prince if you want. You shouldn't
have dragged us into it."

Aunt Dora's eyes narrowed. "Do you remember when
you were about six years old, and you snuck outside after
your bedtime to play in the first snowfall of the season?"

The sudden change of subject threw her, but the memory
was already sharpening into clarity. The night had been
crisp and layered with shadow. Only the slivers of light
from a neighbor's window saved her from tripping over
her own feet as she crept out the back door. The snow
had crunched under her boots. She'd taken off a glove

just for a second to touch it; it had been icy and numbing, nowhere near as soft as it looked, and had turned her skin pink as a burn. Her footsteps left great muddy pits that swiftly disappeared under more snowfall. The part she remembered best was how the clean, cold smell of the air had painted itself into her lungs, freezing her breath before it ever made it past her lips.

"What does that have to do with anything?" she said.

"You came down with a cold the next day," Aunt Dora reminded her. "Your mom stayed home from work to take care of you and missed the arrival of a rail hiker. Everyone else's caseloads were full. So the newcomer was turned away from Brume."

"She—she never told me that," Roda said, with a wave of belated guilt.

"No, and rightfully so—you were only six. You could hardly be blamed. But do you see?" Aunt Dora said. "A child's innocent decision to spend an hour in the snow created a chain of events that, days later, impacted a stranger who never even knew that child existed. Your choice had unforeseen consequences."

"What's your point?" Roda couldn't help the defensiveness that crept into her tone. She knew it wasn't her fault, but she still *felt* responsible.

"Imagine the Prince careening back and forth through the timeline, altering history in both big ways and small ones," Aunt Dora said, drumming the pen against the floor absently. "Even if his intentions are pure—even if he spends all his time rescuing stray dogs and preparing towns for natural disasters—his choices will have consequences no one could possibly predict. And somewhere along the line, he'll make a big mistake, maybe a disastrous one, and he'll have to do damage control. Even *more* ripple effects will come from that. He'll wreak havoc on the world and himself." By now the tapping of the pen was so rapid Roda wanted to rip it out of Aunt Dora's hand. "People aren't meant to go back in time and tinker with history until we're satisfied with the result, because we'll never be satisfied. It's not in our nature, I'm afraid. We're meant to live our lives facing forward."

Roda reached over and placed her fingers on the end of the pen, silencing it. Aunt Dora blinked, as if she'd only just noticed it was still in her hand, and stuck it back in her boot.

"Maybe he has a good reason," Ignis said. "Maybe it's important."

"It does sound kind of dangerous," Roda admitted. She and Mom lived in this timeline, too. She didn't like the idea of the Prince messing around with it.

Will slid the diagram closer and traced the thirty-years-past loop that Roda had drawn with his finger, over and over. She didn't envy him trying to process all this with damaged hardware.

"But it's like you just said. Our choices already have unforeseen consequences." Ignis's hands shook. His voice, too. "What's wrong with doing things over until you get the best possible result? Don't you think the world could be a better place than it is now? But if you don't take any risks, then nothing will ever change."

Roda glanced at Ignis, bewildered by the intensity of his reaction. Then she wondered whether *she* was the one who wasn't reacting right. They were discussing the fate of the world, and all her mind could do was circle around and around Aunt Dora's deception, like a foolish moth mesmerized by a deadly light.

"And how much tampering do you think the timeline can take before it collapses?" The words had no heat to them. Aunt Dora didn't sound like a fearless defender of the timeline. She mostly just sounded sad and tired. "We see time as this eternal, immutable force. But, like any living thing in this world, don't you think it might respond poorly to abuse and manipulation? That it can be wounded, damaged, and maybe even killed?"

Ignis faltered. "Can it?"

"I don't know," Aunt Dora said. "But we can't afford to test those theories. We only get one world. To shred the fabric of time just to see if we can piece it back together a little better is more than irresponsible. It's *unfair*. We don't get to take that risk on behalf of everyone else."

He looked away, but there was a mutinous set to his jaw. He wasn't convinced.

"Nonetheless, you were right before, Ignis," Aunt Dora said. She took the diagram back from Will, folded it up, and tucked it in the pocket of her dress. "We need to get out of here before he comes back."

"You sound like you have a plan," Roda said.

"The plan is to stop him before he steals Nowhere's magical anchor. The anchor holds all the enchantments in place, including the ones that allow the Hall of Time to exist and control Nowhere's passage in and out of our reality. The Prince thinks he can take it and harness its power. But his best chance of doing that is during the short window of time when Nowhere and our world overlap."

An anchor that can't be cast off. She was finally learning what the third riddle from Anonymous had meant.

"Where is it?" she said.

Aunt Dora stood, brushing the wrinkles out of her skirt. "You would've seen it already."

Roda frowned, not understanding. She hadn't noticed any powerful magical artifacts lying around. "So you want to go and get it before the Prince does."

"Yes, but we'll have to make another stop first. Wait here," Aunt Dora said, crossing to the door. "I'll make sure he hasn't left any guards." She crept outside, leaving them alone.

She kept saying "we," like she took it for granted that Roda was going to help her. Roda's head pounded. She was still struggling to wrap her mind around everything she'd just learned. Was she on Aunt Dora's side now? Even though that meant siding with Anonymous, too? She turned to Ignis, opening her mouth to ask what he thought.

Before she could say a word, Ignis got to his feet.

"I'm not going with you."

She couldn't have heard that right. She waited for an explanation, but he only stood there, fists clenched tight at his sides, an unhappy resolve in his face.

"What?" she said, still certain she had misunderstood. "Why *not*?"

He took a breath and squared his shoulders. "I don't

want to stop the Prince. I'm going to help him."

"Are you kidding?" Roda half laughed. "Didn't you hear him? He wanted to lock us up like Aunt Dora."

"He'll let me help him. We want the same thing."

Her mouth snapped shut, teeth clicking together. He was serious.

Anonymous had been his last hope, she realized. He'd been clinging to the possibility that Anonymous was a connection to the family he'd lost. That hope had been dashed, and now he was desperate. Desperate enough to turn to the Prince.

Her eyes prickled with furious tears. "So that's how it is? You'll do whatever he wants, and maybe in exchange, he'll take you back in time to save your family?"

"If it was your mom, wouldn't you do the same?"

She bit her lip, unable to respond. She wanted to say *no, never*, but the truth was that she didn't know.

"Come on," Aunt Dora said quietly. She'd reappeared without either of them noticing. She helped Will to his feet, and they stood together in the open doorway. "This is his choice."

"I can't just leave him!"

"We have to go."

She looked helplessly between Ignis and the door. She

knew she could talk sense into him if only she had a little more time—

Why are you so sure? whispered a voice in her head. *You've never been able to talk him out of anything before.*

And she didn't have time. *They* didn't have time.

"Fine. Do what you want," she said.

"Goodbye, Roda." His voice was so quiet she could barely hear it.

Swiping her sleeve angrily over her eyes, she left.

CH. 23

"PAY ATTENTION," AUNT DORA SAID, AS SHE LED THEM hurriedly through the winding stone hallways and down a new set of stairs. "You might need to find your own way around later on."

She hadn't even said where they were going yet, or why they couldn't go get the anchor right now, and Roda was too angry to ask. Too sick over her last conversation with Ignis.

"How does it feel," Roda panted, jogging to keep up with her brisk walk, "to be—the biggest—liar—in the world!"

"I didn't lie," Aunt Dora said. "I just didn't tell you everything. You're the one who made assumptions."

"Your letter said the poison would make Mom sleep forever. Then you told me that she's fine. Only one of those can be true."

"You should read more carefully," Aunt Dora said, with a maddening smile. "The note said that there is a rare poison that can put a person to sleep forever. It never said I *used* that poison."

"*Perhaps this discussion can wait until we reach our destination*," Will said meekly, clanging along after them.

Roda would've stomped her feet if they weren't otherwise occupied at the moment. "You lived in our house! Where would you have gone without Mom? If only she'd known what you were *really* like."

"Yeah, well, if Mom knew *you* went around blindly trusting letters from complete strangers—"

She was forcefully reminded of how the letters had made her feel special, how they'd appealed to her sense of adventure, how she'd been delighted to have her own secret mystery to solve. Humiliation squirmed through her insides.

"If Mom knew YOU went around writing secret notes to children, like a CREEP, and then POISONED HER, I don't think she'd have had any time at all to be mad at me!"

"*We are going to be overheard,*" Will informed them.

"I already told you, she's *fine,*" Aunt Dora said. "What I gave her isn't dangerous. It's just a sedative. It'll wear off on its own, no antidote needed."

"That's not the point!"

Aunt Dora stopped short. Will bumped into Roda's back, almost knocking them both over. They stood before a closed door.

"Be very quiet," Aunt Dora said. She threw open the door, and starlight spilled inside the corridor, washing over their feet. They were back in the courtyard. Roda's eyes were drawn automatically to the enormous statue of Professor Kader, with his dragon familiar and his clasped hands—

Her brow furrowed as her gaze settled on his hands again. Was he *holding* something?

You would've seen it already, Aunt Dora had said.

Nowhere's magical anchor was right there, hidden in plain sight.

"I thought . . ." Roda said uncertainly. "I thought we had to make another stop before we went to the anchor."

"We do." Aunt Dora pointed at a door across the stony, crumbling plain. It was the door that led to the unlit staircase, the one Roda had bypassed when she'd first arrived in Nowhere. "That's where we're going. Cutting through the courtyard is the only way to get there."

Huge, winged shadows circled the open space. The Prince's guards.

"What are those?" she whispered.

"You'll see. They're looking for you, so you'll have to run as fast as you can. Understand?"

Roda nodded. "But what—"

Aunt Dora pushed her out the door.

A shrill cry sounded from above as Roda half tripped out into the open. She froze instinctively. Soaring over her head, near the glass dome, were three immense mechanical birds. They were obsidian black, with razor feathers and flat red searchlights for eyes. Each beat of their massive wings created gusts of wind that could've knocked Roda over.

Will had said the Prince had given up on making automatons. But he'd been wrong.

They swept through the air to circle above her. One by one, they dove.

The same instinct that had rooted her feet to the ground now kick-started her heart into beating double time. She sprinted across the courtyard. The first of the automatons missed her by a hairsbreadth, crashing headfirst into the ground. She spared a glance over her shoulder, long enough to see it rising from the crater it left in the stone floor, its clawed feet scratching at the rubble. It shook out its bladed wings and fixed its searing red eyes on her.

Aunt Dora and Will had darted out into the courtyard after her. The other two automatons were bearing down on them even as Roda watched.

Her tired muscles burned, but slowing down was out of the question. She wove around a pair of stone benches, leapt over cracks in the ground that would've tripped her, zigzagged blindly until she felt the air shift behind her. She dove to the right. The automaton soared past, missing her narrowly, its sharp wing tips passing inches over her head.

It turned in the air. She stopped and faced it head on as it shot toward her with all the force of a rocket; at the last moment, she ducked. Its momentum carried it well away, and this time, she didn't watch it turn back for her. She was almost there; she raced over the final stretch—

Roda crashed into the door and scrabbled at the knob with numb, shaking fingers. After a few agonizingly long seconds, she flung the door open and collapsed inside, catching herself against the wall to avoid tumbling down the stairs. The door swung loose behind her.

"CLOSE IT!" Aunt Dora roared.

But she was still so far away, and Will lagged even farther behind—

The automaton pointed its beak at the open door and shot at her like a cannon. She slammed the door shut and backed away. The thunderous crash of machine meeting wall made the very ground underneath her shake. But the door held, and then there was silence. It took a moment for her eyes to adjust. The stairs began a few feet away, curving down into the darkness.

Trembling, she forced herself to press her ear to the door. Nothing.

She gulped down air. Seconds passed; her lungs stopped burning and her heartbeat slowed.

But Aunt Dora should've been here by now.

She opened the door a crack. Aunt Dora and Will had barely gotten halfway across the courtyard; Will was cowering under one of the stone benches Roda had passed, and Aunt Dora knelt beside him, trying to coax him out.

The Prince's guards swooped low over Aunt Dora's head. They circled her and Will like a tornado, trapping them. One of them slashed at her with its hooked claw. Aunt Dora rolled away from the bench, dodging the blow, and leapt to her feet. As the three guards whirled around her, preparing for a final strike, her hand fumbled at the cord around her neck. She was trying to get the ring.

What are you doing? Run! Roda thought.

Their black beaks fell open, the hinges creaking. Bright white light gathered in their open mouths, building until it hurt to look directly at them—

A deafening *crack*, a blinding flash. A robotic scream rent the air, crackling and broken and awful, as the guards unleashed all their pent-up power. She coughed at the acrid smell of burning metal. When the spots had cleared out of her eyes, she saw that Aunt Dora had dodged the attack. The blast had knocked her over. She was covered in dust and sprawled over the wreckage of the ground, but already she was pulling herself up, unharmed.

But Will hadn't been fast enough.

She didn't recognize the heap of twisted metal on the ground at first. Only when she made out the two round, glowing eyes staring at her upside down, the metal jaw missing from the skull, did it hit her. She covered her mouth in horror. Will's torso was split open, the sides of the wound jagged, blackened, and pouring out smoke. One of his hands was gone, leaving only a gnarled stump behind. Sparks flew from his ruined frame.

Aunt Dora crawled to him and bent close. She touched

his metal skull and spoke to him, too softly for Roda to hear.

The guards wheeled around in the air, opening their beaks again in preparation for another strike. Aunt Dora made no effort to get away. Her hand went for the ring again, but the cord slipped from her fingers. She was still disoriented from the blast.

If Roda didn't do something—

But why should she help Aunt Dora after everything she'd done?

She froze, undecided, for a heartbeat.

Then she threw the door open and dashed back out into the courtyard. She swiped a chunk of stone off the ground and hurled it at the nearest guard. Her aim was true; it struck the side of its beak.

The guard whirled in the air and fixed its glaring eyes on her.

She found another projectile, threw it, and missed, but she got what she wanted anyway. All three of the Prince's guards lost interest in Aunt Dora, preferring the prey that would fight. Their wings folded back; they shot toward her.

She ran for the next-nearest door, the one to the kitchen, and flung it open. But she didn't go down the steps. She stood her ground. Black and red filled her vision. They were so close she could make out each individual feather, the starlight gleaming down their razor edges—

Seconds before that first arrow-like beak would've pierced her heart, she dove out of the way. The first guard shot past her, through the open door, and into the hallway, which was much too small for its bulk. Its wings crushed into its sides and screeched against the walls. The second guard crashed inside after it, and the third followed, sealing the three of them in. Roda peeked into the staircase and found them stuck halfway down. All she could see was the back of the last guard, its clawed feet scratching at the ground, its crumpled wings squirming uselessly against the walls. They were trapped.

Soft footsteps came up behind her.

"Roda?" Aunt Dora said. "Are you hurt?"

Roda shook her head, unable to speak.

"Come on. There's more of them. We have to get out of here."

She led Roda back to the door they'd risked so much to reach. Roda stopped in her tracks when she caught sight of Will's broken form again. He wasn't moving, and the glow had left his eyes; they were nothing but dark, empty bulbs now. She blinked back tears.

"They killed him," she whispered.

Aunt Dora kicked open the door and turned back to her. The dust made her hair look more gray than white.

"No, they didn't," she said, and opened her cupped palms. There in her hands was a small, glowing wisp, flickering merrily at her. Roda laughed in relief, unable to believe her eyes. Aunt Dora had risked her own life to rescue him.

She smiled, eyes crinkling at the corners.

"That was brave of you," Aunt Dora said. "Running out there like that."

Roda looked away. "What now?"

"We keep going," she said. "It's this way. Come on."

CH. 24

THE CORRIDOR PLUNGED DOWN IN A TIGHT, DIZZYING SPI-ral. Only Will's steady glow kept the dark at bay, and only the patter of their footsteps disturbed the silence.

She thought again of the third and final riddle in her notes from Anonymous. It had mentioned not only an anchor, but also . . .

"Does this lead to the engine?"

"It does," Aunt Dora said.

Roda looked down, but there was no telling how close they were to the bottom of the stairs. She couldn't see more than two feet past the end of her own nose. They were a bubble of light sinking into a black ink sea.

"So Will was right," she said. "Nowhere's not a castle. It's a ship."

"It's both." Aunt Dora pressed a hand flat against the stone wall, an oddly affectionate gesture. "It *used* to be a castle. Professor Kader turned it into something else. Something more."

"How do you know so much about him?" Roda asked.

"I searched for every trace of him I could find during my travels. But there's still a lot that I can only guess. Most historians agree that he came from the northeast region of the Aerlands, near the mountains. He was orphaned at a young age; the books tend to gloss over that bit. It's always a footnote. He traveled to the city that we now call Vicentia, looking for work. His teenage years are a blank, but he ended up joining the mage's guild, teaching at the country's first university, and embarking on research expeditions to all parts of the Aerlands. But he was well established in the academic world before he returned home, to this place."

"To Nowhere."

"Yes, but it wasn't Nowhere yet," she said. "It was his family home. He inherited it from his parents, but he left it abandoned for decades before he finally came back. I guess he must have seen it as the ideal setting for his experiments, since it was empty and secluded." She paused, choosing her next words carefully. "I can't say *why* he created Nowhere. But it tells me something, that when he wanted to experiment with time travel, he returned to a place where he'd suffered a great loss. I know for a fact that the Prince feels a kind of kinship with him. But Professor Kader had a restraint that the Prince lacks."

"So that's what you were really doing, when you said you were on university-funded research trips." If Roda sounded bitter, she couldn't help it. The lies went so far back.

"I *did* work with the universities," Aunt Dora said. "And he wasn't my only research subject. But his work provided a foundation for many of the mages who came after him. Some of his enchantments are still functioning, even after all these years, like the Aerlands' mist. For now."

"The ice dragons," Roda said automatically, and then paused. "What do you mean, *for now*?"

"No enchantment lasts forever. They'll wake up one day." Aunt Dora shrugged, as if the Aerlands' impending doom was of no more interest to her than the weather forecast. Sure, the Traveler had managed to jolt the ice dragon into a momentary wakefulness, but it had fallen asleep again before it could do more than lift its head and huff at Ignis. Probably no one in Brume had even noticed—maybe the mist had shifted, maybe it had shivered, but it would have settled down too fast to cause any alarm. It hadn't occurred to Roda that the dragon could ever wake up *for good*. That it could just . . . fly away, taking the mist with it, and leave Brume exposed and vulnerable. But Trax had told her that outright, hadn't he? He'd said when the dragon flew it would look like a cloud; he'd said it wouldn't fly again *for a very long time*. A long time wasn't *never*. She'd just been too distracted to grasp the full meaning of his words.

"Oh, don't look like that," Aunt Dora added. "There was a time before the mist and there will be a time after. Life goes on."

"What about the train guardians?" Roda asked. Without the mist, they'd be needed more than ever.

"Once they're gone, we'll have to figure something else out."

She didn't sound anywhere near as worried as she should, Roda thought. She remembered the book she'd stolen from the library, hidden in her bag still, and considered telling Aunt Dora about it. But Aunt Dora went on before she could convince herself to broach the subject.

"I studied Professor Kader's surviving enchantments and found pieces of his research stored in hidden bunkers and libraries around the world," Aunt Dora said. "But the bulk of his work is lost—well, not lost. It was here all along."

She sounded wistful. For her, finding the journals in the library must've been like stumbling upon a treasure trove.

For every question Aunt Dora answered, Roda came up with a dozen more. And despite Aunt Dora's assurances that Mom wasn't in danger, Roda wouldn't feel better until she went home and saw her in person. But she couldn't do that until the Hall of Time opened. What was she supposed to do until then, other than stay with Aunt Dora?

Ignis had made his choice so easily. She couldn't blame him, not when he had a chance to get his family back. He'd sounded like he really believed in the Prince's cause, too. Roda knew that she should feel more strongly, that she should share Aunt Dora's urgency to defend the timeline from the Prince. But all she felt was hollow.

The stairs ended at a door, and behind the door was a closet-sized space with a ladder that led up to a hatch in the ceiling. Will cast a golden sheen on the rungs and sent streaks of shadow over the old stone.

Aunt Dora scaled the ladder, hooked her legs through the top rungs to balance, and turned the wheel on the hatch. It resisted at first, groaning so loudly Roda winced—

but at last the hatch popped free. Aunt Dora pulled it open. Pale blue-white light poured down, bathing the ladder room in its haunting glow.

Aunt Dora hoisted herself off the ladder and through the opening in one smooth, graceful motion, like an otter snaking into a river. She popped her head back down just long enough to say: "Hurry up!"

Will drifted after her obediently, fading into the bluish light and disappearing beyond the hatch. That left Roda alone with the dark stairs at her back.

She hurried up.

The cold, thin metal rungs bit at her palms as she climbed the ladder. Getting through the hatch was the tricky part. She pulled herself halfway up over the edge, but then there was a gut-twisting moment when her feet slipped off the ladder and her legs dangled uselessly. A last desperate burst of strength got her upper body through. She crawled the rest of the way in and flopped down on the floor, panting, her cheek pressed against the cool stone.

Aunt Dora's footsteps and her hushed, one-sided conversation with Will sounded very far away. She turned over onto her back, raising an arm to shield her eyes from the light until they adjusted.

The spots cleared from her vision. Her heart jolted in her chest.

Wow.

When she'd heard the word *engine*, she'd pictured a blocky lump of metal, like the kind that ran the trains. Big, rumbling, practical.

Nowhere's engine wasn't anything like that.

A web of machinery arched over her head. Its network of piping widened, here and there, into cylindrical chambers, valves, and pumps. Suspended in the middle of it all, like a heart, was a spherical tank.

This was the source of the light; whatever was inside the tank glowed so brightly it seeped through the metal and ran like luminous blood through the ducts. Despite the fact that it had been around for centuries, since Aurelion Kader's time, it all looked brand-new, gleaming, and somehow alive.

The web took up nearly every inch of the cavernous space. It connected to the walls, floor, and ceiling, transforming the whole place into a three-dimensional maze. The air was cool but charged; the hair on her arms stood on end, and her skin tingled. A low hum came from every direction, accompanied by the smell of burning.

"Aunt Dora?" she said, scanning the room for her. A

weak sparkle in the corner of her eye gave her pause. It took her a beat to realize it was Will. The pale light permeating the room washed him out; he was the faintest blur of gold hovering near her shoulder. "Are you all right, Will?"

Will flickered. Maybe she was projecting, but she thought there was something anxious and fearful in the pulse of his glow.

"I imagine," Aunt Dora said behind her, "it's hard to go from having a physical form to *not* having one anymore."

It wasn't just the light in the room. Will was fading. She hadn't noticed it in the darkness of the staircase, but he was definitely fainter since leaving the automaton than he had been before.

"You think he misses having a body?"

"If I had to guess," Aunt Dora said.

"Can we find him a new one?" Roda asked. She reached out to cup Will in her hands. He attached himself to her sleeve, clinging like a snowflake.

"He *is* one of Professor Kader's wisps," Aunt Dora said softly. "And Nowhere is Kader's creation. His greatest creation, I'd say. I can't think of a better place for him."

Roda jerked around to look at her. "*Here?* The engine? But it's . . . Is it even safe?"

"I believe he'll know just what to do once he's there. He was practically made for this." Aunt Dora studied Roda's face, reading the hesitation there. "It's up to you."

Roda's throat closed, and unexpected tears prickled behind her eyes. Ignis and Will had been through everything with her. She hadn't expected to finish this journey without them. She didn't *want* to.

But she wasn't selfish enough to hold Will back.

"What do I do?" she said.

"Come with me."

They picked their way through the forest of struts and piping, under arches pulsing with that mysterious crystalline glow. Roda followed, covering Will with one hand, somehow nervous that if she didn't keep him close, he'd disappear.

Aunt Dora stopped. They were now well away from the entrance, behind the huge tank suspended in the center of the web.

"There," Aunt Dora said, pointing at the tank. "If we put Will inside, he'll be able to go anywhere he wants within Nowhere."

She hooked her hands over a conduit that swooped past her shoulder and pulled herself up. In seconds, she was a good eight feet off the ground, using the pipes as hand-

and footholds as she climbed through the web.

"You'll need to come, too," she said, pausing to look down at Roda from her perch.

"I—I can't," she stuttered. "I'm not good with heights. I—"

"I know," Aunt Dora said, more gently than she'd spoken to Roda since they'd reunited. "But you won't fall. Trust me."

"I *can't*."

And she wasn't talking about the climb anymore.

"You've done a lot of things you thought you couldn't do," she said. "This is just another chance to prove yourself wrong."

Whenever I had to do something I didn't think I could, Roda thought, *I acted like you.*

There had been so many times, over the last couple of days, when she'd convinced herself to be brave by thinking of Aunt Dora. Now those memories were painful. If she had been wrong to believe in Aunt Dora, then had those moments of strength been an illusion, too?

But she had to do it. For Will.

With a final glare at her aunt, she grasped the nearest part of the web and stepped up onto a pipe curving past her knees. Will hung on to her. Aunt Dora talked as they climbed, answering some of the questions Roda hadn't known how to put into words.

"Nowhere couldn't be constrained by the rules of our reality if it was to work the way Professor Kader needed it to," Aunt Dora began. "The Hall of Time couldn't exist in our world. That's why it's so hard to find this place, let alone get inside."

"But you and the Prince did anyway."

The tank was a solid twenty feet up, and the burning smell intensified as they approached it. Roda wrinkled her nose.

"Yes," Aunt Dora said. "For most people, though, it's impossible. Just like a real comet, Nowhere has an orbit. Except it's not a space rock orbiting the sun, but a pocket universe orbiting our reality. When its orbit brings it close enough to brush our world, that is the *only* time Nowhere is accessible. To even learn about its existence, you have to uncover Professor Kader's most carefully hidden work, which is full of warnings about how dangerous Nowhere's power would be in the wrong hands. Then there's the leaving enchantment, which ensures that those who *do* find their way into Nowhere can't take its secrets back out with them. Professor Kader made sure the key to Nowhere would remain locked away in his mind, even after he died."

"If Professor Kader cared that much, he shouldn't have left it up to chance," Roda snapped.

Then she mentally replayed Aunt Dora's words. That one phrase, *leaving enchantment*, what did that mean? Would something happen to them when they left Nowhere? The Prince had said something about it, too. She racked her brains, trying to recall the conversation she'd eavesdropped on, but climbing took almost all her concentration. Aunt Dora traversed the web with an impressive combination of agility and utter disregard for her own safety; keeping up with her was a struggle.

"Here," Aunt Dora said at last.

She'd found a perch near enough to the tank for her to touch it. There was a door set into it, latched shut. Roda drew level with her on a parallel pipe.

"Will's supposed to go in there?" she said nervously.

"That's right. Go ahead."

Roda looked down at Will, who had been reduced to the tiniest fleck of light against the back of her hand. Will trusted her. And she couldn't let him down. She reached for the hatch and opened the door.

Brilliant blue-white light surged out, fierce and unrestrained. Roda shielded her eyes.

"It's okay," Aunt Dora said. She could have been talking to either of them, Roda or Will.

Blinking through the spots in her vision, Roda lowered her hands. Will drifted up to the opening, a flash of gold so faint she might've imagined it.

"Bye, Will," she choked out.

It was like that was what he'd been waiting for. He drifted through the hatch and disappeared.

"You don't need to say goodbye," Aunt Dora told her. "He's not gone. Look."

Roda ducked her head and peered through the opening.

She gasped. The inside of the tank was like a pocket of outer space. Swirls of silvery particles drifted through the darkness, which was very deep—much deeper than the tank appeared to be on the outside. She couldn't see its inner walls at all.

Even as she watched, that darkness dissipated like shadow under the blaze of the sun. The particles spilled from the hatch, diffusing through the engine room. It was neither liquid, solid, nor air. It was the very essence of light.

"What *is* that?" she breathed.

"Stardust," Aunt Dora said. "It's what makes Nowhere run and powers its enchantments."

The air grew thick and warm, and stung her lungs, as though she were breathing in static electricity. It seemed to seep through the lining of her throat and stomach and infect her blood. As the stardust passed through her lips, it wasn't taste or smell or texture that Roda sensed the most clearly. She had the distinct impression of coming untethered, floating away from Nowhere and into deep space, drifting through the universe with nothing but the stars and the planets and the galaxies for company.

Aunt Dora shook her shoulder. "Don't get lost. I know it's overwhelming—"

Roda coughed into her arm, trying to clear the foreign feeling from her throat. When she looked inside the tank again, it was almost empty. Its inside walls were visible now, metallic, mundane, except for a few patches of iridescence that clung to them like extraterrestrial scuff marks. Other than that, the tank showed no sign of ever having held anything more exciting than gasoline. "If this is what makes Nowhere run, won't it—won't it crash?"

"Let's hope not," Aunt Dora said cheerfully. "But it *will* go on lockdown. The Prince is probably on his way here now."

CH. 25

SICK HORROR TWISTED THROUGH HER GUT.

"You tricked me," she said, angry at herself more than anything else. She *knew* Aunt Dora couldn't be trusted, and yet she'd listened to her anyway.

"No," Aunt Dora said. "You really did save Will."

"But that's not why we came here. You said we had to go to the engine room to . . . to . . . ."

Aunt Dora had never explained it. She kept delivering bits and pieces of information to Roda, just enough to keep stringing her along, but not enough to put the whole picture together.

"Why do you think the Prince has been trapped in Nowhere for ten years, and still hasn't managed to take the anchor?" Aunt Dora said. Roda could only shake her head, too numb and furious to respond. "Because Nowhere's highly aggressive defense system stopped him every time. But during the ten-second window when Nowhere is connected to our world, all its energy is focused on keeping the Hall of Time open; there's not enough spare power to activate the defense mechanisms. That makes it the perfect time to steal the anchor. I stopped him the first night. I stopped him last night, too. Tonight is his last chance." She paused, as if waiting for Roda to understand her genius plan. When Roda didn't speak, Aunt Dora continued in a rush: "But by opening the tank, we've set off Nowhere's defenses and forced his hand. The advantage of waiting is gone. As soon as I'm out of the way, he'll go after the anchor with the strength of an army he's spent ten years building. Nowhere will put up a fight, but it might not be able to protect itself this time. It's up to you to stop him."

"I can't do that!" Roda said, aghast.

"You *can*."

"No! I'm sick of this!" Roda said. Her voice rose to nearly a shriek. "I don't care about Nowhere. I want to know why you did all this, why you lied to me—"

"I told you!" Aunt Dora snapped. "Because I need your help stopping the Prince!"

"*Why?*" Roda asked. "How could *I* possibly help *you?* The Prince can do magic, and you've been on all these adventures and you know what you're doing—"

"How can you still be arguing when you know how important—"

"Why *me?* Why do you need me?" Roda demanded. "And how do I even know you're doing the right thing? Maybe the Prince is the good guy and you're the bad guy! You haven't even told me enough to know what's right or wrong!"

The stardust spilled its unforgiving light over Aunt Dora's drawn, weary face. Since when did she have those thin lines around her mouth? Since when did she have hints of silver-gray in the white hair at her temples?

"Sometimes it's not as simple as right or wrong," she said. "Sometimes every choice you make has a right side and a wrong side."

"Why do *I* need to be the one to make the choice?"

"Roda, look at me. Look at my face."

"I *am!*"

It was only then, with Aunt Dora's features swimming before her, that she felt the tears welling in her eyes.

"Look at my eyes. My nose. My *hair.*" She tucked a snowy lock behind her ear. "Haven't you ever wondered why you look so much more like me than your own mother?"

"Because I look like Dad, and you're his sister," Roda said, voice breaking.

"Dad didn't have a sister."

"Stop," Roda said. "I don't want to hear any more lies—"

"I met the Prince when we were children. He'd just survived a terrible tragedy. So when he and I discovered Nowhere, *together*, he became obsessed with the idea of changing the past," Aunt Dora said rapidly. This was a new version of the story she'd told before, about how the Prince had visited Nowhere three times. Before, she had skirted around her own role in the tale; now, she was laying everything out. "The leaving enchantment made him forget most of what we went through. He remembered the journey that brought us here, but not what happened while we were inside. That's what the leaving enchantment is for—that's how it protects Nowhere. We went home, and moved on with our lives, and—and he was my friend. I wanted to believe he was getting better, recovering from the traumas he did *and* didn't remember. But I was wrong." Grief crossed her face like a shadow. "He knew the comet hid a powerful secret. From there, he learned about Nowhere again by digging up Professor Kader's research and teaching himself mage-script so that he could read even his most arcane work. When he finally returned to Nowhere with the intention of traveling back in time, I followed. *I* went back, too."

Roda shook her head. The tears spilled over, but she cried silently. She felt numb, detached from her body, unable to accept what part of her already knew to be the truth.

"I'm not your aunt," Aunt Dora said. "I'm *you*. A version of you from a future that might or might not happen again. The Prince is Ignis. That's why I brought you here."

"I'd never—" Roda choked out, but couldn't continue.

"One-on-one, I can't beat him. I needed help. *You're* the one who has to stop him. I wouldn't trust anyone else to do it," Aunt Dora said. "I'm sorry I couldn't do more to guide you. If I told you what to do, you'd have just repeated my mistakes. I tried to give you the tools to do what needed to be done, and the freedom to do it *better*. I don't know if I succeeded. As children, the Prince and I never bickered the way you and Ignis do. Even when I was doing my best to pretend I really believed he was a crow, I could tell the two of you were driving each other to distraction. But you still cared. That matters. If you didn't care, you'd never get through this."

Roda took a deep, rattling breath. Her throat and eyes and lungs burned. "I only came here to save Mom," she croaked. "If Mom's okay, then I'm here for no reason."

"I know you don't believe that," Aunt Dora said fiercely.

Somewhere in the distance, a door slammed.

"We're out of time." Aunt Dora pressed a piece of paper into her hand. It was folded around a hard, coin-sized object. Roda took it automatically, clutching it like a lifeline. "He won't be able to see you from here. No matter what happens, *do not move*."

Before Roda could form a response, Aunt Dora was gone, scrambling through the web, around the tank, and away from her.

Tears dripped off her jaw. Her fingers on the pipe were growing slippery with sweat.

This couldn't be happening. Aunt Dora was lying—but why would she choose a lie like this? It made sense. So many things made sense if this was true. Including—it struck her suddenly—how Anonymous had seemed to know the future. Roda had spent the past couple of days fixated on the parts of the letters that contained clues about Nowhere. She'd all but forgotten that the way Anonymous had won her trust in the first place had been by making predictions that had kept coming true. Anonymous had known the future because Anonymous had lived it. Because Anonymous was Aunt Dora, and Aunt Dora was . . .

She couldn't say it even in her head.

A *bang* of metal on stone rang through the engine room as someone threw the hatch open. Roda couldn't see it from where she sat, but she knew who it was.

The Prince had found them.

CH. 26

" RODA! " THE PRINCE BARKED.

Her body went cold with terror. But then the awful truth dawned on her: he was talking to Aunt Dora.

"Up here!" Aunt Dora called. Carefully, Roda moved to where Aunt Dora had been sitting before. From there, she could peek around the side of the tank and see the rest of the engine room.

Aunt Dora hung off the web some ten feet ahead and to the right of Roda. When the Prince turned to her, she beamed, as if delighted to see him.

His white hair was tied behind his neck, but a few strands had come loose around his face. Even from below, he seemed imposingly tall; his plain black garb was striking against the shimmer of starlight, and his eyes were the brightest point in the room.

Ignis was with him.

He already knows who the Prince and Aunt Dora really are, she realized. That was why he'd stayed behind. As soon as he'd seen the Prince in the library, he'd known that he was looking at an older version of himself. From there, it must have been easy to figure out the truth about Aunt Dora, too.

"What have you *done*?" the Prince roared.

"Oh, you know. Spilled a little bit of fuel. Nothing major."

"Do you know what's happening out there?" The cool restraint he'd shown earlier was gone; he was coming undone.

"Nothing good, I'd bet," Aunt Dora said.

"Where's the girl?" He was pacing now, eyes darting around the room, taking in the glimmering trails of stardust still dancing through the air. If he went for the tank, Roda was done for.

"She ran off when I told her the truth," Aunt Dora said. She hoisted herself up easily and swung her knee over so that she half knelt on the pipe, her other leg dangling.

He stopped and stared at Aunt Dora, eyes narrowed. "You told her?"

"I could hardly keep it from her much longer," Aunt Dora said. "Hello, Ignis. Tell me, how are you feeling? Is your future self everything you hoped he'd be?"

Ignis flinched.

"Don't talk to him," the Prince snarled. "Where did she go?"

"I don't know. I told you, she ran off."

"Liar."

"Takes one."

They glared at each other.

"What does she think she's going to do by herself?" he asked. "No, she's smarter than that."

"All I know is that she doesn't want to fight you. Either of you." Aunt Dora laughed bitterly. "She's too young to know better."

"And you came here."

"Since you plan on ripping Nowhere apart anyway," she said, "I might as well help you get started."

He breathed hard through his nose. "Get down from there."

"Or what?"

"Or I'll come and get you!" he snapped, his voice haggard with fury.

Aunt Dora grinned, a little too brightly for someone

who couldn't fly *or* do magic.

"You go ahead and do that," she said.

"*Fine.*" To Ignis, he added: "Search this place. The girl might be hiding here."

Panic surged through her, but then the Prince's transformation almost made her forget the danger she was in. She'd seen Ignis shift plenty of times. But the Prince didn't turn into the little crow that fit snugly in her backpack. He *grew*. His arms elongated, curved, and sprouted feathers as long as her hand. His face was replaced by a cruelly sharp beak. When he soared up into the air at last, changed, he was the size of the automaton guards—the guards that had been modeled after Aethons all along.

So this was why Ignis had kept talking about flying her up the mist, or catching her if she fell off the dragon. Or hunting stags. Aethons could control the size of their shifted form; he was capable of *this*, too.

The Prince beat his powerful wings and streaked toward his target, weaving over and under the silvery curves of the engine with ease. Aunt Dora didn't move until he was almost upon her. She shut her eyes briefly, as if steeling herself. Then she rolled sideways off her perch and fell.

Roda covered her mouth to hold back a scream. But

Aunt Dora caught herself a few feet below, dangling from another pipe. She pulled herself up and ran across a surface not even wide enough to put two feet side by side, balancing as if on a tightrope. The Prince was hindered by his size; there were parts of the web he couldn't reach because the gaps were too tight. But he gained on Aunt Dora as she climbed and leapt and swung through the web, leading him in a chase that took them both farther and farther away from Roda.

The cocky grin was gone. When Roda glimpsed Aunt Dora's face, it was grim. She slowed, faltering, and then sped up and out of Roda's line of sight. Roda clung to the tank, the note in her hand crumpling and growing damp with sweat.

Another set of wingbeats, quiet and close, reminded her that *she* was being hunted, too. Her eyes found a small white blur weaving through the engine. Ignis. She pressed herself against the tank, trying to keep out of sight, but it was too late—he swept around to her side of the engine room, and a golden eye met hers. His flight path wavered just barely.

He'd seen her.

He circled the tank once and flew on.

Roda didn't move. Didn't breathe.

Then Aunt Dora cried out. Roda twisted around to look, fearing the worst—

But the Prince hadn't caught up to her. She'd slipped; she was falling. She hit part of the web with a painful, metallic *thud* on her way down, snatched for a handhold and missed. The Prince dove for her, but he wasn't fast enough. Aunt Dora slammed into the ground with a horrible, sickening *crack*.

CH.27

DESPITE EVERYTHING, THE ONLY THING SHE WANTED IN the world was to make sure Aunt Dora was okay. But her last warning rang through Roda's mind: *Do not move.*

The Prince swooped down on Aunt Dora's prone form, transformed in midair, and landed beside her.

"Roda?" he said, his voice shaky with worry.

Aunt Dora groaned. "That was embarrassing."

"It was reckless!" The concern was gone so quickly Roda was certain she'd imagined it. "What would you have done if you'd snapped your spine, you hotheaded fool—"

"Couldn't you just magic it better?" She propped herself up on her elbow, shook her white curls out of her eyes, and made an attempt at a cheeky grin, though it came out more like a pained grimace. "What, all these years brooding over magic books and you can't even spell a few bumps and bruises away?"

The way she held her left arm against her chest, protectively, made Roda wince. That didn't look good.

"Please shut up," he said, and reached gingerly for her arm. "Let me see that."

"Ow."

"It's your own fault."

"*You* chased me, so it's yours."

"You practically dared me!" he said, in the exact same outraged tone of voice she'd heard from Ignis a million times. Her heart twisted painfully. "It's sprained."

"I'll live. Just help me up."

He stood and held out his hand. She reached up as if to take it—only to snatch at the fingers of his glove, pulling it clean off. He wrenched his hand away, but not before Roda saw it: the Traveler's ring. He'd kept it.

Aunt Dora cackled. "You still wear that trinket?" she said, throwing his own words back in his face. "How sweet."

She wasn't surprised. She'd *known* he still had the ring, because she'd met another version of the Prince when she was twelve, too. Maybe she'd even hidden where Roda hid now.

"Get up," he spat, yanking his glove back and shoving it onto his hand.

She rolled to her feet, a smirk playing over her lips.

Had she fallen on purpose? Had she been following a script remembered from her own childhood, re-creating the actions of another Aunt Dora?

Ignis alighted next to the Prince, shifting in the air and landing on two legs.

"Any sign of her?" the Prince asked.

There was no tremor in Ignis's voice as he responded: "No."

"Look again, and then meet me at the top of the stairs. Quickly."

He sent Aunt Dora down the hatch first. She made a show of struggling to climb down one-handed. The Prince did not offer to help her this time. But he watched her closely, and then he jumped after her, leaving Ignis behind.

The ensuing silence was unbearable.

In seconds, Ignis had flown back up to her. They sat side by side, high above the ground, and if Will had been there, it would've been just like their climb through the mist. Roda didn't know whether she was relieved to see him, or ashamed at the mess she'd gotten them both into. Or angry.

"You covered for me," she said.

He shrugged. His eyes dropped to the note in her hand. "So I guess she told you, then."

"Why didn't *you* tell me?" she said, her voice thin and reedy.

"I didn't know how. I didn't want to believe it myself." He drew in a sharp breath, as if readying himself for a fight. Was that what they were doing? Fighting? Was Ignis supposed to be her enemy now? "You don't have to help her."

"Her? The Prince is the one who's trying to—trying to—"

"Save people's lives? Save my *family*?" Ignis said. "We don't know anything bad will happen if the Prince gets what he wants. It's just what your . . . what *she* thinks. She can't know for sure."

He was right. Was she just parroting what Aunt Dora had said because she didn't have concrete beliefs of her own? How much of what she *did* believe—about everything— was because of Aunt Dora, who'd raised her almost as much as Mom had?

Her head hurt from thinking, her eyes hurt from crying, and her throat hurt from the effort of suppressing the scream bubbling up inside her.

"Roda," he said. "Come with me. Please."

He held out a hand. And she *almost* took it. It would've been the easiest thing, no different from when she'd let him steady her as they'd raced up the ice dragon's back. Ignis had promised not to let her fall. She'd trusted him then. She *still* trusted him.

But she had trusted Aunt Dora, too, and where had that gotten her?

"I—I don't know," she said.

His expression iced over, and his resemblance to the Prince was unbearably clear. "Fine."

He shifted, soared away, and dove through the hatch. Before Roda had fully processed what she'd done, he was gone. And she was alone.

Regret stirred in her, but not for long. Something about being alone allowed her thoughts to burst through the neat little barricades she'd put up to keep herself calm while the Prince had taken Aunt Dora captive. With no one around and nothing to distract her, she had no choice but to confront what she'd learned.

It's not true. It can't be, a small voice insisted in the back of her mind. In the place where her terrors, anxieties, and insecurities lived. Even after everything, that fearful part of her wanted to close her eyes and pretend none of this was happening.

Aunt Dora was Roda's future self. She had gone back in time, created a fake identity, played the part for ten years, and then lured Roda to Nowhere—all to protect the timeline from Ignis. Or maybe to protect Ignis from himself.

Without the threat to Mom's life hanging over her head, Roda never would've put herself through any of this. She could admit that. If Aunt Dora had said, *Help me save the timeline*, Roda's response would've been a firm *No, thanks*. It was one thing to fantasize about going on wild adventures across the world like Aunt Dora had, and another to actually do it. Using Mom against her had been the perfect way to force her hand, and Aunt Dora had known it would be perfect because she *was* Roda.

Roda shut her eyes, and a few more tears squeezed out, making her eyelashes clump together. She rubbed them away with her sleeve.

There was something growing inside her.

It felt a lot like rage.

Maybe Aunt Dora had been Roda, once, but Roda *wasn't* Aunt Dora. Not yet. Aunt Dora didn't get to choose

Roda's fate for her. She didn't get to manipulate her. Just because she'd chosen her path didn't mean she got to push Roda in the same direction. Roda had the right to choose, too.

Aunt Dora wanted to stop the Prince. But what did Roda want?

Mostly she wanted to go home.

But not without Ignis.

Even knowing that Aunt Dora had orchestrated their meeting, it didn't change the fact that Ignis was her friend. He'd ventured into the mist with her, even though it had almost killed him once. He'd saved her from the spirit-hoarder. He'd helped her brave the climb. He'd protected her from the Prince just now, and since she was still free, that meant he hadn't turned her in yet, even after they'd fought.

They were friends. That was real.

And if *she* wasn't Aunt Dora, then *he* wasn't the Prince.

They weren't pawns for their older selves to use in a battle against each other. The Prince and Aunt Dora could have their little showdown without them.

She looked down at her hand, clenched around the crinkled scrap of paper. She knew what it was without opening it: one last letter from Anonymous. Part of her was tempted to rip it up and throw away the pieces, but her curiosity overruled her better judgment.

The hard object wrapped inside the note turned out to be Aunt Dora's ring. She must have taken it off when Roda wasn't looking. Her stomach flipped at the sight of it in the palm of her hand; it didn't belong there.

Why would she give this to me?

Maybe the note would answer that question. But whatever it said, it wouldn't change her decision.

It was only a few lines long. She smoothed it out and began to read.

INTERLUDE

IGNIS WOULD HAVE TRADED THE SPIRIT-HOARDER'S WHOLE treasure trove for a single quill and a scrap of paper.

His mind kept wheeling around what he knew, and what he didn't know, about the timeline he lived in.

Not a line at all.

But a loop.

He *hated* that. He hated it because it was confusing, and he didn't like things that confused him. But he also hated what it meant.

The world as he had known it had ended with the eyrie's destruction. That event had been a kind of apocalypse. For him. For his family. For his people. But a loop meant that this event, which had changed the whole course of his life, was simply a replay of something that had already happened before. It wasn't the first time the eyrie had fallen. It probably wasn't even the second. So how many times had it—

Stop, he told himself. *Focus on what you know.*

Some of it he had guessed, and some he'd been told. He knew that the man he now called the Prince had grown up with the same flock in the same mountains as Ignis had, and *his* eyrie had fallen, and *he* had wound up in Brume and met the girl who would become Aunt Dora. The two of them followed their own Anonymous to Nowhere, and met their own version of the Prince. They'd stopped him and survived, though the Prince remembered none of that part. He had pieced things together, just like Ignis was doing now. But before the Prince had been able to explain *why* he didn't remember—something about a *leaving enchantment*—they'd had to drop everything and race to the engine room.

"Stop falling behind," the Prince snapped, startling Ignis out of his thoughts.

"You don't have to be so harsh with him," Aunt Dora said.

"Stay out of it!" he and the Prince said, at the same time. Ignis looked away in disgust. His eyes dropped, unwillingly, to the Prince's glove, which hid the ring that matched Aunt Dora's.

As a rule, Aethons didn't wear jewelry. The enchantments used to ensure their clothes survived their shapeshifting were nearly impossible to perform on metal, crystal, stone, and other such materials. But they did have a custom of exchanging rings. It had started with the Archon—a ruler from ancient times who'd led the very first Aethon flock. He'd forged and enchanted rings to bestow upon his closest advisors as a symbol of trust and loyalty. When he died, each advisor split off with a few followers, creating new flocks that dispersed across the world. Because they carried the Archon's rings, it was said that the Archon was with each of them, in a way.

The ring-exchange tradition had evolved from that tale. They didn't always signify a romantic bond, and mated pairs weren't expected to wear them. Ignis's parents hadn't. Shifter-friendly rings were just too much trouble to make. But a ring meant: *Find me in your next life.* If you died wearing your ring, the stories said, your soul would remember to wait for your partner before passing on, and then the two of you could be reborn together. Which sounded like a drag for whoever was stuck waiting around in between lives.

It was nonsense, of course. The whole thing about souls finding each other. If they did, he doubted rings had anything to do with the process. It was downright mortifying to see his older self wearing one.

What had he been *thinking*?

Still. His mother would've given him the thrashing of a lifetime if he'd given someone a ring and then stopped wearing it. Or even lied about not wearing it, like the Prince had. Ignis felt a chill, as if Queen Fiera's ghost was hovering over him.

He'd neglected to tell Roda that he'd been royalty. It didn't matter anymore. As the fifth hatchling of King Percutien and Queen Fiera, he hadn't been next in line to lead, and now that he was the only surviving member of the royal family, there was no one left *to* lead. But it was almost funny, in a horrible sort of way. He'd nicknamed their enemy *the Prince of Nowhere* only to learn he really *was* a prince. Because he was . . . Ignis.

Whatever Aunt Dora had done in the engine room had turned Nowhere into a haunted, menacing place. The lanterns had been extinguished by an unseen force. The cleaning enchantments were frozen, leaving feather dusters and mops suspended motionless in the halls. The Prince kept glancing over his shoulder and checking around corners before ushering them on in utmost silence, as if expecting an assault.

Unless he was really that afraid of a missing twelve-year-old girl, there was something or someone else in Nowhere the Prince was worried about. But what?

"In here," the Prince said. He opened the door to a small room lined with cabinets and stepped aside to let Aunt Dora in first. "You stay outside and keep watch."

"For what?" Ignis asked. But the door was already swinging shut, with Aunt Dora and the Prince inside, and Ignis outside, fuming at the sealed room.

He doesn't think I'm just going to stand here, does he?

Ignis turned the handle, agonizingly slow, and opened the door a crack. Just enough to hear what was going on inside.

The Prince's footsteps. Drawers being opened and shut. A hiss of pain from Aunt Dora.

Finally, she said: "When did you learn to treat a sprain?"

"Even Aethons fall down when they're first starting to fly," the Prince said. "We learn basic first aid almost as soon as we're old enough to venture out of the nest."

"Thank you, Ignis."

Discomfort speared through Ignis at the sound of his name.

The Prince didn't respond. After a beat, she said, "You're older. Even though you've been in here."

"The laws of time might not apply to Nowhere, but I still have a mortal body."

"I was wondering if you'd figured out a way around that little problem."

"Not yet."

"Is that the next step in your plan, then? Immortality?"

"My enemies don't get inside information about my plans."

Ignis returned to his mental timeline, still working through it.

In the previous cycle, the-boy-who-would-become-the-Prince had left Nowhere with the-girl-who-would-become-Aunt-Dora. Sometime in the ensuing years, he had decided to find Nowhere again, go back in time, and save the eyrie—and she had followed him. They would have been about twenty-two when they returned to Nowhere and used it to travel to the past. And they'd gone back twenty years. They'd *had* to, because going back only ten would have meant arriving weeks too late to stop the destruction of the eyrie.

When their older counterparts emerged from Nowhere after traveling back in time, Ignis and Roda would have been two years old. Their adult selves had still been friends then. She *had* tried to dissuade him from going back, but once it was done, she had supported his rescue mission. Or so he'd thought. He hadn't realized until much later that when she wasn't visiting him at the eyrie, Roda's counterpart lived that decade as Aunt Dora, splitting her time between her travels and her home in Brume. Preparing to step into the role of Anonymous, if it became necessary. Ignis's counterpart spent those years trying to avert the destruction of the eyrie. But he failed.

Why didn't he ever try to warn me?

"I lied, earlier," Aunt Dora said. The mention of a lie caught his attention, and he focused again on the conversation going on behind the door.

"What else is new?" the Prince muttered.

"You were right. The leaving enchantment didn't work on me. I have a . . . permanent immunity to it."

There was a pause filled by a shuffle and the scrape of a drawer.

"Why are you telling me now?" the Prince asked.

"Because you're going to fail," she said. "And at a terrible price."

"If I'm going to fail anyway, why are you trying so hard to stop me?" he retorted. "Why don't you sit back and watch it all unfold as it will?"

"I don't want to lose you."

"If I do fail," the Prince said, "it'll be because we're at odds. We've always been better together than apart. If you helped me, we could do so much good."

"It's not our job to decide the fate of the world."

"Of course it is! It's everyone's job to build the future they want to see," he said fervently. "But not everyone is lucky enough to have the tools that we do. Roda, we could stop the Vicentian Massacre. We could prevent the extinction of the gryphons. We could go to the future and find a cure for the disease that killed your m—"

"And how do you know those things wouldn't cause even worse catastrophes?"

"If they do, then we'll deal with it!"

The sound of the Prince's voice made Ignis cringe: desperate, like he thought if he could just say the right thing, find the magic words, he'd get through to her.

Had Ignis sounded like that earlier, when he'd argued with Roda?

"It's irresponsible to play around with time," Aunt Dora said. "It's wrong."

"Fine," the Prince said. The fight had gone out of him. "Have it your way. But if you're expecting the girl to finish the job, you're going to be disappointed. I won't let her interfere."

"Don't you *dare* hurt my niece."

The Prince laughed. "Has all this back and forth through time finally broken your mind? She's not your niece!"

"I know that. But you don't understand. I spent so many years trying to give her what she needed to be brave and resilient and curious about the world—it was practically all I thought about sometimes. And I . . . when I was her age, and I learned the truth, I thought it was all an act. That *my* Aunt Dora didn't love me, that she was just using me. But now that I'm on this side of it, I know that wasn't true. I—"

"Save it," the Prince said. "Say what you want about me, but at least I had the decency to leave my younger self alone until I had no choice. I never even spoke to him until I helped him escape the eyrie."

Ignis bit down on a gasp. His mind catapulted him back to the worst day of his life: the fighting in the eyrie's halls, glass on the floor from broken windows, whole rooms on fire from misplaced lightning strikes, the flash of Jaculus weapons and armor. Thick black smoke polluted the air. Dead and dying Aethons lay everywhere he looked. He'd barreled blindly through the eyrie's upper levels, trying to find his siblings. And then a hand had seized his arm, swinging him around and dragging him down a side hall.

Ignis had struggled until he saw the guard's uniform, and then he'd simply surrendered and let himself be led away from the carnage. The man had stayed in front of Ignis; he'd thought it was to protect him, but he realized now it had conveniently prevented him from seeing the man's face.

He'd taken Ignis to one of the eyrie's flight exits, which opened onto a sheer drop, and practically shoved Ignis out of it. *Fly south*, he'd said. And Ignis had. It had taken some time before the panic had worn off, and when it did, it was replaced with shame. He'd turned around and flown back home. But by the time he got there, it was all over.

He'd always thought the guard had simply grabbed the first member of the royal family he could find. He hadn't realized he'd been singled out.

"At least I didn't *brainwash* him into becoming what I wanted him to be," the Prince was saying, while Ignis pressed his back to the wall and tried not to slide to the ground.

"That's not what I did. I wasn't brainwashing her. I was preparing her."

"Call it what you want." In the brief pause that followed, the dizziness passed and Ignis thought he could maybe stand up without using the wall for support.

With this final piece of the puzzle, Ignis's imaginary timeline was complete. After the eyrie fell, and after he'd saved Ignis in his disguise as a royal guard, Ignis's counterpart had returned to Nowhere again. That was when he'd encountered Roda and Ignis in the mist, as the Traveler, aged thirty-two. He had slipped into Nowhere with the intention of staying there and mastering time travel. He couldn't stay in the present, because he would have wanted to avoid Roda, Ignis, and Aunt Dora. He would not travel to the future, because—Ignis could guess this much—that would put distance between him and a time when the eyrie was still standing, and he wouldn't have been able to bear that. He went back in time just ten years, and stayed inside Nowhere, slowly transforming into the person Ignis now knew as the Prince. Aunt Dora didn't follow him that time; she'd stayed in the present. So she was thirty-two still, and he was forty-two.

This meant that Ignis, his adult counterpart living alongside him in the eyrie, and the middle-aged version of him holed up in Nowhere had all existed at the same time.

The Prince said abruptly: "Why didn't you tell me? If the leaving enchantment didn't work on you, then . . . then . . ."

"I didn't want to hurt you."

"And how did that work out for you?" Another pause. "In the last cycle, did *your* Aunt Dora tell *her* Ignis?"

"I don't know."

"Great."

Ignis wished they'd speak more plainly about this leaving enchantment. But they kept blowing right past it, like they didn't want to dwell on it. Already they were moving on.

"You're more ruthless than the last Prince," Aunt Dora said. "Roda told me what you did in the mist. Locking them in the bunker, siccing the cleaner on them, waking the dragon—*we* never had to deal with that."

You didn't? he thought. But something must have happened to them in the mist, because they'd still ended up with white hair. Was that purely coincidence, or were some things fated to happen no matter what else changed?

"I'm not more ruthless. I'm more desperate," the Prince said quietly. "This time, the invasion at the eyrie . . . It was worse."

Ignis held his breath.

"Worse?" Aunt Dora said.

"Last time, there were survivors. This time, none, except me and the boy. I spent ten years working on peace negotiations between the Aethons and the Jaculi, and it

260

amounted to nothing. Worse than nothing." He gave a hollow laugh. "I can't leave things like that. I can't."

This time, Ignis had to sit down. He pressed his forehead to his knees and tried to keep his breathing steady.

It didn't have to be this way. He didn't have to be the only survivor.

His heart was torn between fury at the Prince for meddling . . . and hope. If the Prince had changed history once, then it could be changed again.

"I see," Aunt Dora said. "So this is really it."

"It is."

As footsteps approached, Ignis hastened to get up and move away, to make it less obvious that he'd been listening; the Prince was coming back out. A moment later, the door swung open.

"Wait," Aunt Dora said. The Prince paused at the threshold. Ignis could see her moving nearer over the Prince's shoulder.

"What?" the Prince said, half turning back to her. That was all the time she needed.

Something flashed in Aunt Dora's hand. Ignis had no time to cry out a warning before she plunged a pair of surgical scissors into the Prince's side. With a choked gasp, he staggered against her. His hands flew to her shoulders—

Ignis didn't know whether he was trying to push her away or cling to her. She blinked back tears.

Ignis was paralyzed with horror.

"I'm sorry," she whispered to the Prince. "I had to try."

She wrapped her good arm around him and moved to guide him to the ground, but he shoved her away. She stumbled back into the room, bloody and dismayed.

The Prince yanked the scissors out with a trembling hand. They clattered against the tiles. His palms pressed over the wound, stemming the blood; he leaned heavily against the doorframe.

"Why?" he rasped.

"I—" she stammered. "I was trying to change what happened next."

"By killing me?"

"By escaping!"

He kicked the scissors across the floor to her. They left vivid red streaks on the tiles. "Go on, then. Finish it."

He held his arms open in invitation.

When she didn't move, the Prince looked back at Ignis. His gaze pinned him in place as surely as a nail in his wing.

"Grab the suture kit," the Prince ordered. "She won't touch you."

The words barely registered. All Ignis could do was

stare at the growing damp spot on the Prince's shirt.

"Now!" the Prince snapped.

Ignis skirted around the Prince and into the room. Aunt Dora couldn't even look at him. His shaking hands rifled through a couple of drawers before he found what he needed. He grabbed it and fled, and the Prince shut the door.

The Prince made it part of the way down the hall before he sank to the ground. Ignis stood over his crumpled body.

He'd never thought of himself as looking much like his parents, but the man before him resembled his father so closely even Ignis would've had trouble telling them apart. The Prince shed his gloves, which were soaked through, and tossed them away. His hands pressed down on the wound in his side again. The ring was black with blood. As Ignis took in the bowed head, the cuts and swollen knuckles in the overworked hands, the unkempt hair and clothes, his prevailing emotion was disgust. He'd gotten *old*. He was alone and barely presentable, a poor reflection of what a full-grown Aethon should be.

"Well?" the Prince said, in a voice harsh and ragged with pain. "Are you going to help me stitch this up, or not?"

The suture kit wasn't too different from what he

would've used at the eyrie, except the instruments were made of metal instead of bone. He got to work.

"Can't you go any faster?"

"Hold *still*," Ignis said. "I don't want any scars."

"I have some bad news for you," he said gravely.

Ignis gritted his teeth and concentrated on keeping the needle steady.

"Aren't you going to ask?"

"I don't want to hear about whatever ugly scars I'm going to have in the future," Ignis said without looking up. These stitches were going to be *pristine*.

"Not that," the Prince said. "Aren't you going to ask how she and I got to this point?"

He wanted to ask. But he was afraid to hear the answer.

"It doesn't matter," Ignis said. "It won't happen to me and Roda."

"Are you sure about that? I would've said the same thing when I was your age."

His fingers hesitated over the bloody, half-stitched wound in the Prince's side. It was all too easy to see himself becoming the Prince. But he couldn't imagine Roda turning into the woman he'd met earlier. Aunt Dora was cold, calculating, and had a steely confidence. A battering ram of a person. But Roda was his friend. She nursed injured crows back to health. She cared enough to ask an irritating wisp its name and teach it to speak. She was kind. She was good and compassionate and she wouldn't hurt anyone. Especially him.

Would she?

"Forget about her," the Prince said. "I can bring back the ones who really matter to us. Our people. Our family. You'll help me, won't you?"

"That's why I'm here." He tied off the final stitch and wiped his bloody hands on the Prince's cloak. "Why didn't the . . . leaving enchantment . . . work on her?"

The Prince scowled. "I don't know how she pulls off half the things she does. No one else, in all my research, has managed to avoid it. She must have found some kind of loophole. That would be just like her."

He sat up and straightened his ruined shirt. At least it was black; the stain was nearly invisible. Ignis *hated* stains.

"So every time you come here and leave, you forget all about it?" he said. "The enchantment does something to your memory?"

The Prince nodded. "But you don't forget anything you knew *before* you stepped through the door. When I came back the first time, I only stayed in Nowhere for a moment, long enough to find the door I wanted and leave again. I had done enough research to expect something like the Hall of Time, and I was able to guess how it worked. As soon as I left, I forgot exactly what it was like, but since I'd gotten to the time period I wanted to be in, that confirmed my theories were correct."

"If we fail," Ignis said, "I'll have to start from scratch. Like you did."

He'd forget that time travel was a possibility. He'd have to rediscover it all alone. Maybe with Roda working against him.

"That won't happen," the Prince said. "But from here on out, you must obey my every command."

Ignis nodded. He couldn't let the Prince fail. He'd do whatever it took to save his flock.

A small part of him wavered, thinking back once again to his last conversation with Roda in the engine room. She'd refused to help him. But she'd hesitated. He was *sure* she'd hesitated.

That conversation hadn't been all that different from the way Aunt Dora and the Prince had squabbled. Except *their* argument wasn't a new one. No, they'd had the same discussion before many times over—that was plain from the tone of their voices. By now, they should've given up on each other. But they hadn't. The Prince still wore that pointless ring. And Aunt Dora had faltered when faced with the prospect of killing him. Ignis hadn't failed to notice that the stab wound was shallow and had missed the Prince's vital organs. Would he and Roda wind up like that, locked in a never-ending battle, not only for the timeline but for each other's loyalty?

One of them had to budge, eventually.

But it couldn't be him.

The Prince walked away, moving carefully but gaining speed. Ignis trailed along at his heels until the Prince stopped abruptly.

"Do you hear that?"

Ignis listened.

It was faint but unmistakable: the padding of soft footsteps, accompanied by the whisper of a tail dragging over the floor. Then voices, speaking in the sibilant tongue of his people's enemy.

Horror closed around his throat like a fist.

There were Jaculi in Nowhere.

CH. 28

THE LETTER WAS PRINTED IN THE SAME DISTINCTIVE handwriting Anonymous had always used. Roda would have recognized Aunt Dora's dramatic, looping script, so it made sense that Aunt Dora had disguised it for the notes. Or maybe *this* was her natural style, and Aunt Dora's writing had been the disguise all along.

It began as all the others had: *Dear Roda*.

If you want to hide, stay in the engine room. You can wait there until the Hall of Time opens again.

If you want to find me, go back to the room where the Prince locked me before, turn right at the next corner, and knock on the second door on the left.

If you want to stop the Prince, go to the courtyard.

What she actually wanted was to find Ignis, and Ignis would be with the Prince.

It was infuriating. As soon as she wanted to be rebellious and disregard Aunt Dora's instructions, Aunt Dora decided not to give her any instructions to rebel against. And she hadn't mentioned the ring at all.

If you want to stop the Prince . . .

Did she, though? Even if she wanted to—could she? Her first thought had been to turn her back on Aunt Dora and the Prince's feud. She should never have been involved in it, anyway. But if what Aunt Dora had said was true, about the damage the Prince could do to the timeline, then *everyone* was involved. Not just her. Mom, too. Mr. Worrel and Nylla and her other friends at school. Trax the train guardian, the sleeping dragons, every person and place Aunt Dora had ever told her a story about. The whole world. Except Roda was the only one in a position to help, and . . . if you could help, then you *should*. Mom believed that. Roda had always thought that she believed it, too, but—she didn't know anymore.

Finding Ignis was her first priority. She would decide about the rest later.

She climbed off the engine, through the hatch, and back up the stairs. Her flashlight's beam cut through the eerie, celestial glow of the stardust drifting up from the engine room.

What had Aunt Dora done? What defense system had she triggered?

The journey back up was lonely. She wished Will were with her. His familiar golden light would've been a comfort.

The hair rose on the back of her neck. She whirled around and pointed her flashlight down the stairs.

No one was there.

But she was *sure* she'd felt something. A presence on the outer edges of her senses.

She swallowed her fear and took the final few steps at a jog, refusing to look behind her again. Her light shone on the door to the courtyard. Sounds filtered through it: crashing, shouts—

She threw the door open and stopped short.

It was like she wasn't even in Nowhere anymore. The walls, the floor, the glass dome and the stars beyond— they were gone. Bright white sunlight blinded her.

When her eyes adjusted, she stood on rocky soil with mountains rising all around her. The air was cold and crisp, and the sky was the palest blue, and the world was endless. There was no mist. Before her, the ground sloped gradually down. A blot of green far away—a forest, maybe?—blended into a gray-white horizon. Streaks of pink and yellow lingered in the sky, the tail end of a sunrise. Behind her, a sheer cliff went up so high she couldn't see the top of it even when she tilted her head all the way back. Its crown disappeared into the clouds.

The only remaining sign of the courtyard was the statue of Kader and his dragon. Even now, it was no less imposing than it had been the first time she'd laid eyes on it.

The screams she'd heard were clearer now, and with them came the boom of thunder, the flash of lightning, the roar of fire. The wind smelled of blood and smoke. Something terrible was happening above her, high up on the cliff, beyond the shroud of cloud cover. If Ignis was up there, she didn't stand a chance of reaching him.

"Ignis?" she called. "Ignis! Where are you?"

She made her way to the statue, trying not to lose her footing; the ground was steeper than it looked. Her boots sent loose rocks skipping and rolling down to knock against the statue's plinth.

Why is this the only part of Nowhere I can still see? she wondered. She stood at Kader's feet and peered up into his ancient, carved face. The dragon's eyes seemed to follow her. She shivered.

Her gaze dropped to Kader's hands, folded in a relaxed, dignified way that suited his stately posture. But Aunt Dora's letter had confirmed her suspicions: *If you want to stop the Prince, go to the courtyard.*

The anchor was here, hidden in Professor Kader's grasp. And the Prince was probably on his way to retrieve it right now.

But why hadn't he gotten here yet? And where were those screams coming from?

Another sound distracted her before she could follow that train of thought further—a door, opening out of thin air. It was only a slit in the canvas of the world, at first, framed by two craggy outcroppings that leaned together like a pair of crones trading gossip. As the door was shoved open, the slit widened, and the canvas . . . *wrinkled* around it, so that she could almost see the rest of the courtyard again, its weathered walls and its star-strewn sky. Two people stumbled through the door. It slammed shut behind them and then was gone, taking the rest of the courtyard with it.

It's all fake, she realized. They really *were* still in the courtyard. Everything she thought she was seeing, even the mountains and the sun, was an illusion.

The Prince saw her first. Against the soft, pale colors of

their surroundings, he was living shadow and night. His black garments were torn. His hand covered a wound in his side, and his face was streaked with blood and soot. When his eyes met hers, his lips pulled back in a vicious, fanged smile.

"So there you are," he rasped, his voice hoarse as though he'd been screaming. "The timeline's last hope. I was wondering where she'd stashed you."

She didn't bother answering him. The Prince was a kind of illusion, too. Just like these mountains. Just like Aunt Dora: a persona, not a person. He was made of borrowed power and dreams of a timeline that didn't exist. He had spent his life chasing an imagined reality.

In all of Nowhere, Ignis was the only thing that was real.

Her eyes found him now, half-hidden behind the Prince. If she could get through to him, he'd see it, too—that they were better off together than apart. But his face was blank. He looked straight through her. She might as well have been invisible.

And then a body fell from the sky.

CH. 29

A WINGED SHAPE PLUMMETED FROM THE CLOUDS AND crashed between her and the Prince. Dirt and pebbles sprayed out in every direction. It skidded down the slope, trailing wet black feathers and leaving streaks of dark blood behind, until it finally came to rest a few yards away.

It didn't move again, not even to twitch. Its wings, broken and limp, stuck out crookedly. Roda clapped her hands over her mouth, feeling sick.

It was an Aethon.

An agonized cry tore itself from Ignis's throat. He staggered toward the corpse, but the Prince grabbed his arm.

"It's not real!" the Prince said, giving him a rough

shake. "Focus! They're coming back—"

"Ignis!" she shouted.

He didn't seem to hear her. His glassy eyes were fixed on the dead Aethon and full of open, unguarded pain, like the whole world was collapsing around him.

The Prince made a sound of disgust and released him. Before she could call out again, another Aethon slammed into the ground. This time, the Prince wasn't fast enough to stop Ignis from throwing himself on his knees beside the cadaver, reaching out to stroke its feathers with trembling fingers.

"Ignis!" She closed the distance between them, slowing when she started to slip, flinging out her arms for balance before running on. "We're still in Nowhere. This isn't really—"

This isn't really happening, she wanted to say, but even if the dying Aethons weren't real, the way Ignis felt about them *was*. The Prince wasn't even looking at him anymore; he was—

She stopped, following his gaze. There was nothing to see, at first, but the leisurely drift of feathers as they voyaged slowly downward. Despite the din from above, the silence there in the mountain pass was as still and perfect as the surface of a pond.

But Aethons didn't just drop dead. Something was killing them.

As if responding to a command, figures emerged from crevices in the granite slopes and the caves that pockmarked the cliff. They slipped out of hiding places above and below, leaping to the ground from high-up perches. Sunlight gleamed off their armor; their weapons of bone and wood and stone cast long, pointed shadows.

Then the nearest one turned, and she saw that what she'd mistaken for armor was actually a hide of diamond-patterned scales. Shining green and blue and black and yellow, the scales covered their bodies, from their smooth heads to their clawed hands and feet. They did wear armor on their torsos and lower bodies, but it seemed more decorative than anything else, adorned with polished bone medallions. Their beady eyes had vertical slits for pupils; under their flat noses, forked tongues flickered out of fanged mouths to taste the air.

She shuddered. So these were Jaculi. The creatures that had killed Ignis's flock.

He was still crouched beside the dead Aethon, smoothing out the mussed feathers in its wing. Now, more than ever, she knew she'd been right to come back for him. She couldn't let him face this alone.

The Prince bared his teeth as he faced his enemies. He raised his clenched fists before him and then flung them apart. A wave of power exploded from his slim profile, a stream of lightning that slammed into the ten nearest Jaculi soldiers and blasted them away. Their bodies landed, burning, in the dirt.

The rest of the Jaculi charged him all at once. He leapt into the air, sprouting feathers, and soared out of their reach. Their arrows and javelins followed him.

But he wasn't alone. He had an army, too.

The courtyard doors flashed into view for an instant as they were flung open, and the Prince's automatons streamed through them. They dove at the Jaculi, clawing at them with their wickedly sharp iron nails and slashing with their beaks. Even flightless, the Jaculi did not make easy targets. They threw their weapons with deadly accuracy, piercing the automatons in their eyes and in the gaps where joints connected, and sending them crashing to the ground. The ringing of metal on metal, the *crack* of lightning and the roar of flame, the screams of dying Jaculi and damaged automatons—it all melded together, deafening.

Roda skirted around the worst of the battle; the Jaculi paid no attention to her. At last, she knelt beside Ignis.

Very carefully, not wanting to startle him, she laid a hand on his shoulder.

"Ignis, it's me."

Slowly, his head turned. His eyes widened, as if he was surprised to see her there. "Roda?"

She smiled reassuringly. "Yeah. Are you okay?"

"I don't—" He looked down at the black feathers sticking out between his curled fingers. Gently, she tugged his hands away and folded the wing over the Aethon's body. He wiped the drying tear tracks on his face with his sleeve.

"You remember where we are, right?" she said. "We're in Nowhere. None of this is real."

"It is real," he whispered.

"What do you mean?"

"This—" he said. "This is the day that—"

The words were thin and choked, as if they'd had to fight their way out of his throat.

A horrible suspicion dawned on her then.

"Is this the day your flock was killed?" she asked.

He nodded once, sharply. "It's how Nowhere defends itself. By using my past—the Prince's past—against us. Making us relive our worst memory."

"*Why?*"

"To stop him," Ignis said, "from getting to *that*."

278

He pointed at the statue. The Prince's brilliant white form was never far away from it, but any time he came too close, a Jaculus soldier was there to fend him off.

What had made Aunt Dora think that Nowhere needed Roda's protection? How was she supposed to make a difference in a war between a time-traveling Aethon mage and the defensive enchantments created by possibly the most powerful magical being who'd ever existed?

But then the Prince wheeled away from the statue and landed nearby, a rush of wind from his wingbeats washing over them and ruffling her hair. His long white mane had come loose and fell in sweaty clumps around his shoulders. He bore the injuries he'd gained in his winged form—a cut on his forehead, a puncture wound in his thigh. But he barely seemed to feel the pain. The only emotion she could detect on his face was rage.

"This is your fault," the Prince said.

He stalked toward her across the shredded ground, marking the bloody soil with his boot prints. His eyes blazed brighter and more furiously than the false sun.

"You did this. You triggered Nowhere's defenses."

"That was Aunt Dora." She stood and backed away.

"There is no Aunt Dora!" he snapped. "It's just *you*. It's always just been you."

"Wait," Ignis said, getting to his feet. "No, wait—"

"I'm *not* her!" Roda said, raising her voice.

"You are."

She should've been afraid. But mostly she was just angry.

"Don't tell me who I am!" she howled.

He held his fist out in front of him, and then—she didn't know how it happened or where it came from. His hand was empty, and then it wasn't; a long, thin blade grew from an object half-hidden in his grasp, lengthening until it was at least three feet long, like an enormous iron needle. He gave it an expert flip, changing his grip and holding it at his side like a sword. Crackling white light sparked up and down the blade, throwing harsh shadows over the planes of his face.

It wasn't a sword at all, but a lightning rod. The Prince's fingers were curled around a hilt of deep, shining blue.

Iron with a blue stone.

The ring.

"Stop!" Ignis grabbed his arm, trying to hold him back. But the Prince shook him off with ease and knocked him clean into the dirt. Ignis's head slammed against the ground. He groaned in pain and did not get up again.

There was no one else to stand between her and the Prince.

"Think of this as payback," the Prince said softly. His free hand briefly touched a bloody spot on his side. Lightning billowed off the blade; it sent jagged white lines crawling up his arm, sang in the voice of a whip-crack and spat out sparks.

In the background, somehow audible even over the din of the battle, was a deep rumbling sound, as if the very mountains were murmuring warnings to her.

"You can't do this," she said, with more conviction than she felt. She shoved her hand in her pocket, closing it around Aunt Dora's ring. "You *won't*."

"Are you sure about that?" the Prince asked. With the point of the blade, he traced a diagonal arc through the air, leaving behind a searing afterimage. By now the entirety of the blade was sheathed in lightning, so concentrated she couldn't look at it directly. The full force of that blast would kill her. Would kill *anything*.

She clutched the ring so tightly it dug into her palm. She didn't know how to make it change, or if it *could* change, but Aunt Dora must have given it to her for a reason—

Please be another sword.

The Prince advanced on her. She couldn't hear his footsteps over the hum of the lightning-charged blade, could barely see him past its blinding brightness.

Help me! she thought.

The ring's weight and shape changed in her hand; suddenly she was holding something very large, so large it bowled her over, and she was on the ground, arm held defensively over her head and tucked through a set of straps attached to a large, round disc—

Aunt Dora's ring wasn't another sword. It was a shield.

There was a *boom*, a flash that drowned the whole world in white, an impact on the shield that sent a painful recoil up her arm and made her teeth vibrate. But when the light faded, she was still alive.

She scrambled to her feet, the weight of the shield almost unbalancing her again. Sunlight glinted off its sapphire face.

Through the spots in her vision, the havoc unfolding around her, she found the Prince. Lightning zinged over his blade once more. Roda tensed, preparing to duck behind the cover of her shield, wondering how many strikes it could take before it cracked.

"Do you think you're going to stop me, Roda?" the Prince said, the hum of the lightning rod mingling with the low growl of his voice. "All by yourself?"

The rumbling she'd noticed earlier crescendoed into a groan, a sound that should've signaled an impending landslide—but it wasn't coming from the mountains after all.

"*No*," said Professor Kader's statue, as he stepped off his plinth. The dragon slithered off his shoulders, and as its scales glinted, Roda recognized that metallic sheen for what it was: stardust. "*I will.*"

Nowhere's last line of defense was Professor Kader himself.

CH. 30

"YOU'VE NEVER TALKED BEFORE," THE PRINCE SAID, WITH a mirthless smile. "I liked you better quiet."

Kader's every step made the world tremble. As his hands moved, Roda searched for a glimpse of whatever it was he held—the mysterious object Aunt Dora had called the *anchor*. But he cupped it to his chest protectively before Roda could catch more than a glint of light.

With his free hand, Kader made a sweeping gesture at the Prince. The dragon of stone and stardust took flight.

Its serpentine body slithered into the air, cutting through clouds of dust and feathers. Its tail lifted off the ground, dragged up Kader's side with an awful grinding noise and a shower of sparks, and flicked—with a grace stone shouldn't have been able to achieve—as it swept off his shoulder. Those vigilant silver eyes fixed on the Prince, sighting its target; its back arched, and its jaws opened in a snarl, and it prepared to dive.

The Prince transformed and shot skyward, flying as high as he could. Roda couldn't see the courtyard's glass dome, but she knew it was still there, and the Prince stopped short of hitting it. His opponent gave chase. There, against the pale sky of a day long past, the Aethon and the dragon weaved around each other in a fight that more resembled a dance.

Professor Kader's likeness watched from the ground, so still that Roda would never have guessed he could move if she hadn't seen it herself. He must've been commanding the dragon silently, somehow. This, then, was why the Prince had failed to steal the anchor before now. Why he'd dedicated himself to learning magic and building an army for ten years. Why he'd wanted to wait for Nowhere's most vulnerable time before making another attempt. Because Professor Kader protected the anchor not only with ancient enchantments, but with his own two hands.

She ran to where Ignis lay sprawled in the dirt. He'd hit his head, but there was no blood, only streaks of mud in his white hair. If he could've seen himself, he'd be mortified.

When she shook him, his eyes opened a crack. He squinted against the sun.

"Are you all right?" she asked.

He sat up, blinking dazedly. "Are *you*?"

"Yeah. Professor Kader stopped him."

"Professor . . . ?" His voice trailed off as he took in the sight of the statue displaced from its plinth and the Prince's battle overhead. Then his eyes fell to the shield still strapped to Roda's arm. He mumbled something that sounded like, "*That explains it.*"

"Let's go," Roda said. "I only came back here for you."

"You shouldn't have," he said miserably. "You could've gotten hurt."

"Do you still want to help him? After what he just did?"

"I—I don't know what else to do."

His voice was so small the din of the battle nearly overwhelmed it. But even if she hadn't heard the words, his defeated expression said more than enough. She wanted to tell him that their part in all this was over—that all they had to do now was hide, wait a few hours, and escape Nowhere together.

She *wished* she could tell him that. But something held her back.

The Prince had tried to kill her just then. He hadn't even flinched. It was only now starting to sink in. If not for the shield, she would've been struck by lightning and burned to a crisp. What would happen if the Prince got what he wanted? If he controlled Nowhere's enchantments, would Roda and Ignis be able to evade him until the Hall of Time opened? Would he just let her go? Probably not. And then Ignis would never get away from him, either.

Aunt Dora thought that Roda could make a difference here. And what if she was right? People changed each other's lives all the time without even realizing it. A mechanic mounted a gear into the control panel of a brand-new automaton and tightened it just right; long after the mechanic died, that automaton taught forgotten history to a pair of children. A miner dug up a chunk of gold that was later forged into a coin, and one day, that coin was melted into a doorway to trap a spirit-hoarder in a basement. A girl played outside in the snow one night . . .

Ripples from the past were everywhere she looked. Knowing that, the idea that she couldn't make a difference was more unbelievable than the possibility that she *could*.

No one would know her name or what she'd done here. No one would blame her if she ran or celebrate her if she saved the day. But they would feel the impact of what she did, whether they knew it or not.

"We . . ." She sighed. "We have to stop the Prince."

"I can't give up on my flock," Ignis said, sounding almost like his normal, obstinate self.

"Don't you want this to be over?" she pleaded. "Don't you want to go home?"

"I don't *have* a home."

"You do as long as I'm around," she said.

Above them, the Prince's army converged on Kader's dragon, latching on to it with their claws and stabbing with their beaks, until it was buried under flashing iron wings. They bore the dragon to the ground, its sinuous body twisting and sinking under their weight.

The Prince was free to dive at Professor Kader's statue. But the Jaculi swarmed it, shielding it with their bodies and launching a barrage of arrows at the Prince. He dodged with ease, circling closer and closer to the statue, but couldn't find a clear path to the anchor in Kader's hand. The surviving automatons left the dragon alone and went to his aid.

The dragon lay on the ground. Puncture marks and jagged cracks from the automatons' assault littered its body. From its injuries rose traces of luminous dust, like translucent blood.

Could a stone dragon die?

One of its eyes opened, then, as if it had heard Roda's thoughts. Its glassy silver gaze met Roda's with unmistakable intelligence.

"Are you going to help me or not?" she asked Ignis.

"I—I don't—" He wasn't looking at her. And she couldn't wait for him to make up his mind.

She left him there and went to its side. Brume's ice dragon could've used this one as a chew toy; still, it was large enough to swallow a grown man whole. Its body stretched away in ribbonlike curves. Standing upright, Roda was level with its pupil, a vertical slit that reflected back her own face.

"What do I do?" she asked, hoping—believing—it would understand.

The dragon made a rumbling noise in its throat. Its head lifted off the ground as it slowly pulled itself upright, rising until it towered over her. She inched backward, unnerved by its sheer size. A sound behind her made her jump, the drag of stone over the ground; its tail had swept around to lie at Roda's feet.

The dragon tilted its head and surveyed her with an expression that seemed to say: *Well? What are you waiting for?*

Readjusting the strap on the shield so that she could sling it over her back, she took her first hesitant step onto the dragon's tail. And then another. This dragon had no ridge down its spine; there was nothing to hold on to, and she had to avoid the cracks in its hide. Halfway up, a bit of stone crumbled away under her boot, and she almost slipped. There was no Ignis to grab her hand if that happened this time. But she didn't stop. She put one foot in front of the other and climbed steadily up coils of scales that glittered like the cosmos. It flattened out its body as she ascended, making it easier for her to balance, until she had reached the top of its head and could hold on to one of its horns.

"I'm ready," she said. Across the ruined landscape strewn with the wreckage of fallen automatons, Professor Kader's statue was buried under a roiling mound of jewel-colored scales and feathers that stuck out like steel thorns. She shuddered.

The dragon's body shifted underneath her, and a scream tore from her throat as it launched into the air.

CH. 31

RIDING A DRAGON FELT A LOT LIKE BEING ON THE ROOF OF a speeding train. The wind whipped Roda's hair back and made her eyes sting and roared in her ears. Her stomach lurched with every shift in the dragon's flight path. All she could do was cling to its horn with sweaty hands and try not to get thrown off.

The Prince's army formed a solid wall in the air, their wings interlocking, their bodies blocking the statue from Roda's line of sight.

The dragon did not slow down.

"Wait," she said, but the wind swallowed her voice.

The automatons' furious red eyes were the only things she could see clearly. Their bodies melded together into one mass, an iron tsunami poised to crash over her, but their eyes seemed to multiply, until there were a million of them glaring down at her. Their cries were sharp as glass, stabbing into her ears. She clung to the dragon's horn with both hands and crouched down, head bowed so that her face was hidden in the space between her outstretched arms—

The dragon rammed headfirst through their barricade. Roda's heart stuttered at the violent jolt of impact; pain slashed and sliced at her from every direction as stray feathers rained down. Thin tears opened up in her clothes, everywhere the shield didn't cover, blood trickling down from cuts underneath.

Then they were clear. The warm sunlight hit her skin, and when she straightened, Professor Kader's face was tilted up at her in welcome.

His stone-carved eyes glowed faintly gold. There was something familiar about that color, that light. But what—?

A *crack* split the air, and the dragon rolled to dodge a bolt of lightning from the Prince. Roda screamed and hung on with all her might. But luck was on her side: the dragon's momentum kept her mostly in place until they were upright again. She shook her hair out of her eyes, scanning the cliffs. A winged shadow passed overhead—the Prince was above her. Crackling energy gathered at his wing tips.

"GO RIGHT!" she shrieked. Amazingly, the dragon obeyed, dodging the next attack just in time. Lightning struck the ground with a blue-white flash and a clap of thunder. It left behind a black scorch mark.

As the Prince's army regrouped and joined his assault, lightning rained down on Roda and the dragon, filling the air with the smell of burning. The dragon spun, swerved, and dove in maneuvers that made Roda dizzy and breathless—but not a single blow landed.

And then Roda saw it: an opening.

Professor Kader turned his head to meet her eyes, and the space between them was clear for a few precious seconds. The hand clasped to his chest reached out to her, and his fingers opened, and there in his palm sat a shining glass sphere.

"NOW!" she cried.

The dragon needed no more instruction than this. It pointed its nose at Professor Kader and shot forward like an arrow, tilting into a steep dive that made Roda certain she would float off its back and be lost to the skies. She wrapped her arm tight around its horn and freed her other hand so that she could reach out, stretching as far as she dared—

The Prince got between them and Professor Kader, throwing himself on a collision course with the dragon. But his eyes were on *her*. He meant to knock her off her perch.

The dragon twisted away, and the Prince missed her by mere inches, his wing tips brushing her hair.

The anchor, she thought. She looked back over her shoulder. Professor Kader's hand was still outstretched, but the glass sphere he'd offered her was gone.

An eerie silence fell over the pass. The dragon alighted on the ground. Around them, Jaculi flickered out of sight one by one, like candles sputtering out. She searched for the Prince, but in the rubble and the clouds of dust and the writhing of injured automatons, she couldn't see him.

The dragon slithered up Professor Kader's shoulders, situating itself around him in its usual resting position. Roda was level with Professor Kader's face now.

"Where is he?" she asked. "Where did he go?"

She hadn't expected an answer, but Professor Kader spoke once more, a single word:

"*Rooooh . . . da . . .*"

"Will?" she whispered.

He didn't respond. But she knew. She remembered releasing Will into Nowhere's engine. Remembered the invisible presence she'd felt in the staircase. This was why none of the Jaculi had harmed her, why the statue had intervened to protect her from the Prince's attack, why the dragon had carried her on its back so trustingly.

Just as Will's spirit had possessed the automaton in the kitchen, now Will's spirit was part of Nowhere.

"Give it to me!" the Prince yelled, and Roda looked up and found him at last. He was with Ignis. The Prince drew closer, but Ignis backed away, his hands clutched protectively around something . . . something that reflected light through the gaps between his fingers. . . .

Ignis had the anchor.

What was left of the Prince's army flew circles in the air, awaiting his command. But the Prince didn't dare set them on Ignis, not when he was holding something so precious.

"Don't do it!" she pleaded.

Ignis looked up at her, and then back down at the Prince, eyes wide.

"You have to promise not to hurt us," Ignis bargained.

The Prince lunged at him. Ignis ducked out of the way and held up the anchor threateningly, as if to smash it on the ground. The Prince stopped, panting and furious, and put a hand up in surrender. His other hand pressed against the wound in his side, which had bled through his shirt.

"I won't hurt you," he promised, his voice a breathless rasp, his eyes fixed hungrily on the anchor, his fingers trembling with the effort of keeping still. "You'll be okay. Everything will be okay. I'll make sure of it."

"Ignis," she said. "Please."

It was such an inadequate thing to say. She had no assurances to give him. She could make no guarantees. She didn't even know what she wanted him to do. Her heart lodged painfully in her throat. If Ignis handed over the anchor, then she hadn't just lost this fight. She'd lost Ignis, too.

He glanced at her, too fast for her to read his expression, and turned back to the Prince.

"What . . . what will you do with it?" Ignis asked. "After you save our flock. Then what?"

The Prince's smile, then, was so dazzling that even Roda was tempted to believe whatever he said. Years melted off him. She saw the Traveler in him again—saw Ignis in him.

With a feverish, unshakeable conviction, he said: "We can do whatever we want."

A calm came over Ignis that matched the hush of the mountains. A stillness. The uncertainty vanished from his eyes, and a familiar stubbornness took its place.

"I'm not turning into you," he said, and flung the sphere to the ground, where it shattered.

CH. 32

A WAVE OF PURE MAGIC LASHED OUT FROM THE BROKEN
sphere; it electrified the air and sent up gusts of wind
gritty with dust and dirt.

Roda shielded her eyes. When she lowered her arm,
the illusion of sky and mountains was gone. They were
back in the courtyard, the glass dome and the blackness of
space arching over her head, the flagstones blackened and
broken from the barrage of lightning attacks. The fallen
automatons lay strewn across the floor in pieces. Those
that were left made wobbly landings, as if disoriented.

At Ignis's feet, the glass shards of the sphere twinkled
under the starlight. From the pieces rose ghostly images:
of a green valley speckled with wildflowers; of a time when

Nowhere was sunlit and bursting with life; of Professor Kader himself, younger, standing beside two people who, from his resemblance to them, could only be his parents.

"It's just a memory box," the Prince said, staring at the shards with mingled shock and fury. "All these years, the thing you've been protecting was a worthless little memory box?"

He whirled around to face the statue. Roda shrank back behind the dragon's horn.

"Where is it?" the Prince shouted. "Where's the real thing? *Where is the anchor?*"

Lightning gathered in both his hands, wrapping up and down his forearms like gauntlets.

Frantically, Roda patted the top of the dragon's head. "Um, hello? Can you get me out of here?"

The Prince took a step; flagstones split under his feet. Lightning swirled around his body and crawled over his neck and face in tendrils like cracks in his skin. He was a living storm. He made a gesture like he was drawing a sword from the air, and the lightning rod materialized again in his clenched fist.

And the dragon wasn't moving.

Roda turned around, wished for luck, and half slid, half fell down the coils of the dragon's spine. She skidded down its tail and dropped about five feet off the ground, landing in a graceless heap.

Then Ignis was there, grabbing her hand and dragging her out of the way. An earsplitting *crack* tore the air. The Prince's power blasted through the lightning rod and swallowed up the statue from top to bottom; Roda screwed her eyes shut against the brightness, but Professor Kader's outline was seared into her eyelids.

"*WHERE IS IT?*" the Prince roared. He struck again.

And again.

And on the third strike, the statue rumbled as if to wake once more. The Prince stood at its colossal feet, blind with rage, and did not notice when hair-thin fissures appeared all up and down its surface. The statue tipped forward. Chunks of it fell away, and at last, with a groan, it toppled. The crash reverberated off Nowhere's walls, so it seemed to go on for ages. Roda and Ignis huddled together with the shield over their heads as pieces of flying debris bounced off its surface.

When it was over, a heavy silence blanketed the courtyard. Ignis got unsteadily to his feet and staggered to the pile of rubble where the statue and the Prince had been. He threw himself onto the mound, digging furiously.

She bit her lip. "I don't think—"

"There's no way I'm dying like *this*," he said.

Moving to help him, her foot struck a large piece of debris, and she nearly stumbled. It was Professor Kader's hand. One of the fingers had broken off, but the rest were intact, loosely curled and rendered with such precision she could even see the fine lines in his palm. His head lay a few paces beyond. It had landed on its side, facing her, eyes aglow.

She knelt beside it. "Will? Are you still in there?"

A fissure appeared in the top of the statue's skull. It widened into a gap, the sides splitting apart and uncovering a hidden compartment. Light spilled out and over the shattered flagstones. There was something *inside* it.

Aunt Dora's words came back to her then: *Professor Kader made sure the key to Nowhere would remain locked away in his mind, even after he died.*

The gap stopped expanding, as if the mechanism for revealing it had gotten jammed. She used the edge of the shield to pry it open all the way and squinted into the light. Her eyes couldn't make sense of what was inside. It distorted under her gaze like the mage-script in Kader's journals. But Roda had breathed stardust and recognized the feeling this object gave her: of being simultaneously untethered and connected to everything in the universe.

This was more than stardust, though. Its power was more intense, more concentrated.

Aunt Dora had said that Nowhere existed outside their reality. If Nowhere wasn't bound by the laws of Roda's world, then maybe it could contain an actual star *here*, within its walls, condensed and compressed to such an extent that Roda could reach down and hold it in her hands. If she dared.

This was it—the anchor to Nowhere's enchantments, including the ones that allowed the Hall of Time to exist. Not stardust, but the essence of a star itself.

"Roda?" Ignis said. He tugged the Prince from the rubble. The Prince stirred and shifted, his face screwed up in pain.

"I . . . I found—"

"What?" He pushed at the Prince's shoulders and propped him up against a chunk of stone that might have once been Professor Kader's thigh. Scowling, he left him there and turned to Roda. "Is that—"

"I think so," she said, putting the shield down.

The Prince bolted upright, blinking blood out of his eyes.

"No!" he roared. But it was too late. Her fingers brushed the burning-hot object, and time stopped.

Ignis was paralyzed midstep. The Prince's teeth were bared in a frozen snarl. The few automatons that were still in flight hung suspended in the air, starlight glinting off their petrified wings.

Only Roda was free, and there was no space in her head to marvel at the totality of the change around her. She held time itself in her hands. Past, present, and future unfurled before her. She could have reached down and plucked the timeline like a string. She could pinch seconds between her fingers; scoop up handfuls of months as easily as cupping water from a river; reach into days past and days that would not happen until long after she and all her loved ones had died.

She could do anything, go anywhere. The power was overwhelming and absolute.

Roda, said a voice. The voice wasn't sound, though. It was a whisper inside her own mind.

"Who said that?" she asked aloud.

You know me, said the voice.

"Will," she said, breathing a sigh of relief. "I'm glad you're okay."

Yes, said the voice. *You saved me. You gave me a new life.*

"Why did you give this to me?" she asked, hands still

cupped around the star. It burned her palms; blisters opened on her skin, bright searing spots of pain, but she couldn't make herself let go.

I didn't want him to have it. It's not his, said the voice that was both Nowhere and Will.

"I don't want it, either," she said. "I don't even know what to do with it."

There are things I can fix, the voice said. As if to demonstrate, pieces of rubble floated into the air and reattached themselves to the walls. The pits in the flagstones smoothed over. Even the statue's plinth and the dragon's tail slowly emerged from the dust. Nowhere was going to heal itself. Or perhaps it was simply reversing time, putting things back to the way they had been before.

But there are some things I can't fix, the voice said. *Like the Prince.*

"People *can't* be fixed," she said. "It's not that simple."

What can't be fixed can still, sometimes, be saved. You know this. You protected Ignis when he would have frozen to death in the mist. You climbed into the engine so that you could deliver me safely into a new vessel. You stood up to the Prince. So I am asking for your help one more time.

"None of that was . . ." She stumbled over her words.

"You make it sound like . . . But I wasn't really thinking when I did any of that."

It doesn't matter what you think, the voice said. *It only matters what you do.*

"Just tell me what you want, Will," she said, frustrated.

Ignis knows enough about Nowhere to find his way back, even though the leaving enchantment will take away his memories of what happened here. He could start the cycle all over again, just like the Prince did. If Ignis returns, then you must return, too, and stop him.

Her heart sank. Nowhere was asking her to become Aunt Dora.

"But you heard him!" she argued. "He made the right choice—he's not like the Prince—"

He will forget. But the anchor to all of Nowhere's magic is there in your hands. Holding the anchor gives you a direct connection to it—it makes you part of the enchantments, in a way, part of the Hall of Time and the cleaning spells and the leaving enchantment, too. You are not a target of the magic anymore; you exist in its foundations. Like me. You can choose to remember, and with that knowledge, maybe you can end the cycle.

"Then I can make Ignis remember, too," she said.

Try.

So Roda tried. With the same newfound senses that had opened up all time itself, she discovered the webs of enchantments surrounding her—and was lost. The magic was everywhere, in intricate patterns and knots that twisted through the air and clung to the walls. Her eyes blurred and her mind did, too, just trying to make sense of even one enchantment. She shook her head to clear it, and with each rough shake, glossy strands of magic fell away from her like spider silk caught in her hair. The threads of the enchantments that touched her moved when she moved; she could pull them away and free herself. But Ignis was across the room, miles of magic between them. An experienced mage like Kader might have been able to sort through these endless configurations of magic, find the part of the leaving enchantment that Ignis was tangled up in, and set him free, too; but Roda was no mage. What she'd learned from the kitchen spells still held true: she didn't know the rules.

She tried to stand and take the anchor to Ignis. But she was stuck on the ground, anchored as effectively as the enchantments were.

Do you understand? the voice of Nowhere said. *My creator's work is not so easily undone. You can free yourself because you are the one who holds the anchor. Not him.*

"So give him the anchor instead," Roda said desperately. "Just for a little bit."

I can't do that even for you.

Because Will wasn't just the wisp who had been both her and Ignis's friend anymore. The longer he had possessed the automaton, the more he had become the automaton; now, he was slowly becoming more Nowhere. Professor Kader had made sure Nowhere could, and would, protect itself at all costs. And regardless of how Will felt, Nowhere didn't trust Ignis.

Her eyes burned. It wasn't *fair*. Ignis had made a choice, and it was going to be taken from him.

But she had a choice, too. She could remember for both of them.

"How many times has this happened?" she asked, uncertain she wanted to know the answer. Aunt Dora said she had gone through all this as a child, and Will had used the word *cycle*. How many times had this cycle repeated itself?

Many times. Do you want to see?

She thought it over for a minute, or perhaps an hour, or perhaps a day. The timestream pulsed around her, alive, and all its other days breathed through her. She experienced them as a whole, like how when it rained she was more aware of the storm than the stray droplets that dampened her clothes. She saw all the people of the Aerlands and beyond, all their pasts and futures woven together, all the ways that even the slightest change could unravel them.

She'd lived in Brume her whole life, and she hadn't understood how big the world was. She'd known, from her books, but it hadn't been real to her.

"No," she told Will. "There's only one thing I want to do."

Change something?

"Make us go forward," she said. "Just a few hours. I want this to be over. I want to get out of here and go home. And—if you can, unlock the room Aunt Dora's in. She needs to come with us, too."

It is done.

She felt time shift around her like currents in a river, dissolving the hours that remained between now and midnight. With Will's guidance, she freed herself from the remnants of the leaving enchantment. And when time unfroze, Roda had five minutes before the Hall of Time would open again.

Five minutes before she could go home.

CH. 33

THE ANCHOR WAS GONE.

If not for the blisters and burns it had left on her palms, she would've been convinced she'd imagined the whole thing. She didn't know where Will had hidden it. She didn't want to know. Professor Kader's head and the sapphire shield rested at her feet.

The Prince struggled to rise, only to fall, wheezing, back into the rubble. Ignis left him there. His eyes flicked over the courtyard, brow furrowed in confusion.

"What just happened?" he asked, turning to her. "*Something* happened. It feels—different in here."

"We're going home," she said.

"But it's not time yet."

She shook her head helplessly. "You'll see."

Aunt Dora burst into the courtyard, panting as though she'd sprinted there. She ran to the Prince's side, barely glancing at Roda and Ignis, and threw herself down beside his bleeding form.

"Nice plan," she said, carefully sliding an arm under his shoulders and moving his head from the rubble to her lap. "Very effective. Perfectly executed."

"I hate you." He turned his head away to cough; flecks of blood sprayed into the dirt. "Am I dying?"

"You'd better not," Aunt Dora said. "I know how fast you Aethons heal. Keep it together, Ignis."

Her hand hovered over the wound in his side but did not make contact.

"Don't . . . go," he whispered. "Don't go."

"Shh," she said. Aunt Dora's eyes scanned the wreckage, lingering on the glass shards nearby, before coming to rest on Roda. "You didn't have to destroy the memory box. That was kind of excessive."

"I—I didn't," Roda said.

"I did that," Ignis said sheepishly.

"*You* did?" Aunt Dora said. "But last time—"

She broke off and stared meaningfully at Roda. With a jolt, Roda understood: the Prince, as a child, hadn't made the same choice as Ignis.

Roda glanced down at the sapphire shield, its shine dulled by a layer of dirt. She still didn't know where the Prince and Aunt Dora had gotten those rings, or why. But she didn't *need* to know that story. The shield was Aunt Dora's, and Aunt Dora's journey wasn't Roda's. It was another lifetime. Another cycle. A knot of dread in her chest loosened—the dread that ending up like Aunt Dora was inevitable. That her fate was sealed. It wasn't.

A door appeared on the far side of the courtyard. Ignis went straight for it and threw it open, revealing the jade-tiled Hall of Time.

They had ten seconds to get out.

"Come on!" he said, waiting for her at the door.

She made to follow him, but Aunt Dora didn't move.

"You go," Aunt Dora said. "I'm staying."

Nine.

"No!" Roda said, horrified. "You'll—you'll be stuck here for ten years, you'll—"

Eight.

"I knew it might come to this," she said. "I've made my choice."

The Prince had passed out, a limp hand wrapped loosely around Aunt Dora's.

"But—"

Seven.

"Go," she said.

"Why would you do this?" Roda choked out.

Aunt Dora looked down at the Prince's crumpled form. "He's not strong enough to move right now. And I'm not leaving without him."

Six.

"No, I mean—" Roda said. "If we hadn't met, none of this would've happened. Why did you—"

If Aunt Dora had done all this to stop him, then why write the letter that had brought him and Roda together in the first place? It wasn't that she regretted saving Ignis, that day he'd landed in Brume. She would never regret that, no matter what became of the two of them.

Maybe that was her answer.

But Aunt Dora said: "If I told you, you wouldn't believe me."

And she smiled that enigmatic smile of hers, the smile that Roda would never see again.

Except perhaps, one day, in a mirror.

Five.

"Go!" Aunt Dora said again, and Roda did.

She followed Ignis into the Hall of Time, and found the

door that was still partially ajar from when they'd come in. Beside it, the door the Traveler had used to go back in time swung open, too, distinguished only by the white feather on the floor in front of it. She caught its handle and pulled it shut.

Four.

She had to warn Ignis.

"After this, you won't—the leaving enchantment—"

"It's going to make me forget everything that happened inside Nowhere." His eyes met hers in a look of peaceful acceptance. Of course: he was used to losing things. "But not you. Right? Somehow, you're going to remember."

She nodded miserably.

Three.

"If I made the right choice once, I can do it again." He took her hand. "Don't let me turn into him. Please."

"I won't," she promised.

Two.

The howl of the wind met them at the door. Past the edge of the tiles, columns of mist dotted the countryside below. She spotted the widest one right away—the capital bursting through the horizon like a white fist. Orienting herself using Vicentia, she found one that from this distance was the breadth of her pinkie finger, and she pointed it out to Ignis.

"Aim there. That one's Brume," she said.

"If I forget where we're going?"

"I'll remind you."

One.

They stepped out of the castle, into the icy embrace of the sky, and fell.

Just like that. Solid ground under her feet one moment, then nothing but the night and harsh winds buffeting her the next. The sky roared in her ears. Her free hand, outstretched like a wing, caught the cold in her palm, and her eyes blurred as the wind stung them. Her stomach swooped, like that moment her foot missed the next step down on a staircase but drawn out for ages, for an eternity—

"Hold on!" Ignis said, barely audible over the wind. His hand in hers disappeared, and she hardly had time to register the feeling of falling all by herself before a mass of white feathers exploded from his frame. Moonlight gleamed off wings twice again as long as she was tall. He caught her on his back, and she buried her fingers in the silky down under his outer bristles. When he looked over at her—with an expression that, even on his avian face, was undeniably smug—his fiery golden eye was bright as a miniature sun.

She could pinpoint the moment when the leaving enchantment took hold. The beating of his wings faltered, and his flight path wobbled; his beak slashed this way and that as he looked around in confusion.

The wind wiped away her tears and tossed them into the night.

"Ignis!" she called. He glanced back over his wing again, quickly, and a flash of relief crossed his eyes. "Over there!"

The flight down was shaky; he must have been disoriented, having found himself in midair with no recollection of how he'd gotten there and inexplicably exhausted to boot. By the time they had cleared the top of the mist and were within Brume's borders, they were half gliding, half falling in a downward spiral. Somehow, still, he was strong enough to guide them to her neighborhood, to her house, and then they were crashing into her weed-choked front yard. Her fence still swung open; the streetlights and birch trees stood their placid watch. Everything was just as she had left it.

I hope no one was looking out the window, she thought, a little hysterically. The rough landing had knocked her off Ignis's back; she rolled over in the grass, rattled but unhurt.

Beside her, Ignis shifted back into human form.

"What *happened*?" he said. "The last thing I remember—"

Passing out after meeting the Traveler at the top of the mist. That would be his most recent memory; everything after that had been erased by the leaving enchantment. She swallowed past the lump in her throat. She didn't know how much to tell him. Not yet. She had to think. And—Mom. She had to check on Mom.

"Wait in the living room," she said, and then dashed into the house. Down the hall, to the kitchen—

Mom wasn't there. In a growing panic, she flew up the stairs and checked Mom's bedroom. It was empty. So was Aunt Dora's. She threw open the door to the last room in the hall, her own.

Mom looked up from where she sat on the edge of Roda's bed, holding *The Magnificent Tales of Willow the White Wolf*. Her lip trembled.

"You came back," she said.

"When did you wake up?" Roda asked.

"About an hour ago. I thought— I don't know what I thought. She never told me she was going to take you with her," Mom said, her voice breaking. "Is she gone?"

Roda nodded, unable to speak.

"So you know, then," she said.

Roda couldn't hold back any longer; her face screwed up, and a sob tore itself from her throat. Mom set aside the book and held out her arms. Roda crawled into her lap and wept against her shoulder for a very long time.

CH. 34

RODA HADN'T THOUGHT ABOUT HOW SHE WOULD EXPLAIN Ignis to Mom. Would she have to tell the whole story from the beginning? Get Ignis to shift back into a crow and keep their old charade up? But it turned out not to be a problem. Mom had known the truth about Ignis all along. She'd only pretended not to because Aunt Dora had asked, promising she'd understand why later.

It wouldn't have been surprising if Mom was upset at the sight of him, or even angry. But she only gave him a sad, sympathetic look and said, "We have a spare room now, if you want it."

Aunt Dora's room.

He elected to sleep on the couch. Roda was supposed

to go to bed, too; it was closer to morning than midnight by then, and Mom said they could all talk tomorrow. So Roda went. But she promptly snuck back downstairs to see Ignis. She found him sitting under the windowsill where he used to sleep with his arms around his knees, brow scrunched in thought.

"The ice dragon knocked me out," he said. "And then we were falling. Did we even make it to Nowhere?"

"Yes," Roda said, and then she hesitated.

The memory of Ignis finding Professor Kader's notes resurfaced: how a desperate hunger had seemed to overtake him, how difficult it had been to pull him away. In retrospect, the beginnings of obsession were obvious. If she didn't tell him about Nowhere, maybe she'd never have to see him like that again. But the Prince had forgotten and still returned.

If she *did* tell him, could she do it with total honesty? Could she bear to tell Ignis that he'd had to watch his flock die again? Could she describe the way his older self had tried to kill her, or the way *her* older self had manipulated them? Could she explain the things she didn't understand herself, like why Aunt Dora had stayed in Nowhere with the Prince?

It was too much of a mess for her to wrap her head

around, and she didn't know if she could tell the story truthfully and in its entirety. And if she didn't tell it truthfully and in its entirety, then she turned it into a lie. She turned into a manipulator, just like Aunt Dora, telling Ignis only what she wanted him to hear, only what it would take to make him do what she wanted him to do.

"It's . . . it's not clear," she said, to buy herself time. "I remember making it into Nowhere. And I remember just before we left, Aunt Dora was there. She was Anonymous all along." All of that was true. She pushed down the guilt and finished with, "I think Nowhere did something to our memories."

When they'd first met, Ignis had pretended he couldn't remember anything. Now, she was the one pretending.

Ignis drummed his fingers against the floor. "It's just so—"

"Unbelievable?" she finished.

"Infuriating! What do we do now?"

"I think it's over," she said. "Aunt Dora stayed there."

Stop calling her Aunt, she thought, and then: *I'll never see her again.*

Pain stabbed at her chest. Even knowing that there *was* no Aunt Dora, not really, she still missed her. She missed the person who had told her stories of faraway places and adventures, who'd helped fill her room with maps and books, who had always made her feel like anything was possible. Now, she was gone, and Roda didn't know if anything about her had ever been real.

Ignis snorted. "I hope she got whatever it is she wanted from us."

"I don't know if she did."

Suddenly, he brightened. "You let me fly you back down! I told you I could."

"You *did* crash, though."

"I never promised a smooth landing."

They slept until afternoon, missing school. Mom would've let her stay home another day or two, but Roda wanted to keep busy. She wanted to move on. Ignis agreed, though he spent most of class the next day staring out the window, deep in thought and quieter than he'd ever been.

It took him three days to tell her he was leaving.

Frankly, she was surprised he held out for that long.

He'd been restless in Brume from the moment he'd gotten there. He was never going to stay longer than he had to. She knew that. But it didn't stop her from trying to convince him, even though she never said outright that was what she was doing. She'd drop little hints into their conversations: *Maybe Nylla, Darin, and Rasheed can come over this weekend,* she'd say, or *It's almost the holidays—wait till you see how pretty downtown is with all the decorations up.*

Reasons to stay, deposited at his feet like fallen feathers.

But once he decided to leave, he wasted no time. He was setting out at dawn, he said, when it was light enough to fly but not so bright that the sun reflected off the mist and made it harder to navigate through.

"You don't have anywhere to go," she argued weakly.

"There are other flocks," he said, more animated than he'd been in days. He glanced in the direction of the stairs—it was late, and Roda had again crept into the living room when she was meant to be asleep. His voice dropped to a whisper. "Maybe I can find them. Maybe—I don't know. I have to do something. I can't just move on like nothing happened."

"Maybe moving on is the best thing to do."

"I have to see what else is out there."

She held back a shiver, seeing already the first traces of the Traveler in him. The words *don't go* sprang to her mind, echoing from a starry, out-of-reach place, but she didn't speak them. Ignis had to make his own choices. And she would make hers.

She still hadn't told Ignis the truth about what they'd

been through. She needed to be alone with what had happened, at least for a little while, until she had sorted it all out in her head.

And *then* she would tell him everything. Every last detail. That was what she'd decided.

Aunt Dora had tried to fix this and failed. Now it was Roda's turn. This was her first test, her first step forward. She didn't know if she was doing the right thing, or if this would be the mistake that ensured the cycle continued. If it would take another Roda and another Ignis to end it for good. All she knew was that his choice mattered. *This* Ignis mattered.

"We'll see each other again," he assured her.

"When?" she said. "When are you coming back?"

"I didn't really plan on giving myself a deadline," he said, exasperated.

"A month?" she suggested. "Three months?"

"Who says I have to come trotting back here? Why don't *you* come with me?"

Another memory from Nowhere surfaced: the two of them in the engine room and Ignis saying, *Roda, come with me. Please.*

She blinked it away. "I will, someday. But only if you come back in . . . four months?"

"I might have to search all over the world!" he said, stretching his arms wide before letting them fall. "I'll need more than four months."

"Then *you* tell *me* when."

He thought it over, tugging at a piece of his white hair— he'd nearly had a meltdown when he'd noticed it, and it had been such a relief to see him acting so normal, upset over something so trivial, she'd almost cried.

"Six months," he said finally. "Give me six months, and then I'll come back home. For a little while, at least."

Home. He didn't even seem to realize he'd said anything special. And maybe he hadn't. Maybe she was reading too much into it. But Roda had told him once that he always had a home as long as she was around. She could only hope that some part of him, deep down, somewhere deeper even than where memories were kept, still knew that.

"Fine," she relented. "Six months."

"And by then you'll be ready for another trip."

"A trip? Is that what we just did?"

"And if you're not," he said, undeterred, "I'll come back six months after that, too. As long as you swear it won't be in vain."

"It won't."

For now, though, Brume was where she needed to be. Roda had school and Mom to think about, and she still hadn't decided how much of Aunt Dora's path to follow.

She wouldn't mind being a *little* like her. Maybe she could find what was left of Professor Kader's writings. There might be clues about Nowhere hidden in Kader's bunkers—his *time capsules*, the Traveler had called them. Within those clues could be the key to saving her and Ignis from Aunt Dora and the Prince's fate. Besides, it wouldn't hurt to see the world if there was a chance she'd one day be stuck in Nowhere herself.

Was the Prince even alive? Or was Aunt Dora all alone right now?

Speculating on that gave her a chill, so she stopped. Instead, she reminded herself of the broken memory box. She remembered the book she'd stolen from Nowhere's library, now hidden safely under the loose floorboard in her closet.

Its title read: *On the Assembly, Repair, and Conditioning of Mechanized Servicemen.*

It was a manual on the train guardians from *before* they were train guardians—from when there was no mist and they were made to be soldiers. The information in that book *might* be enough to make sure no more of them were lost. Maybe even enough to build new ones.

Even if Roda failed to save Ignis, even if she turned into Aunt Dora and he turned into the Prince, she could preserve this success. This knowledge wouldn't be lost again. One small, good thing had already come out of their time in Nowhere: a small thing that might become a big one, with ripple effects felt far into the future. A small change becoming a big change, maybe even becoming a whole new future, starting with her.

This time is already different.

Ignis was too impatient to sleep. Roda stayed up the rest of the night with him, and at dawn, she opened the window. He leaned over the windowsill, poised to transform. But then he paused and looked back at her.

"Thank you for saving me," he said. "I should've said that sooner."

"You saved me, too." She hesitated, not wanting to say the word *goodbye*. "When you do come back," she said instead, "I'll have a story to tell you."

Seconds later, Roda was alone, watching a golden-eyed bird soar over rooftops toward the mist and the sky beyond, until there was nothing left of him but the memory of sunlight on white wings.

ACKNOWLEDGMENTS

WRITING A BOOK CALLS FOR MANY HOURS OF SOLITUDE, but publishing one is a team effort. I am lucky enough to have had the most incredible team working with me on *The Prince of Nowhere*.

My fantastic agent, Erica Bauman, saw the potential in this project before anyone else did. Her editorial insight, level-headedness, and support throughout this journey have been invaluable to me. My brilliant editor, Megan Ilnitzki, helped me pull things out of this story—out of the characters especially—that brought it to a whole new level. It's a much better book now than it would have been without her suggestions, her questions, and her dedication to her work. I can't thank either of them enough.

The Harper team is the best of the best, and I'm thrilled to have been able to put my debut novel in their capable hands. Thank you to Caitlin Lonning, Alexandra Rakaczki, Janet Rosenberg, Lana Barnes, Parrish Turner, Emma Meyer, Lena Reilly, David DeWitt, and to illustrator Carly A-F for her stellar work on the cover. There are so many people working behind the scenes to put new books out into the world and make sure they find their readers, from sales and production teams to booksellers and librarians. All of you have my eternal thanks.

My friends in the writing community have kept me company on my best days and kept me going on my worst. Meg Long, for one, is the first person I go to with news, good or bad. You've fielded probably thousands of all-caps DMs from me, read literally all my work, and talked me off numerous ledges. Luck, timing, and possibly supernatural intervention have put us side by side on this journey, and I'm beyond thankful for that, and for you.

My longtime critique partner, Rachel Morris, was *The Prince of Nowhere*'s very first reader. Rachel, thank you for the vent sessions, the memes, the *Buffy* speed-watch, and for being the most amazing friend and CP. And I'm forever grateful for the rest of my early readers: Chad Lucas, Emily Howard, and Mindy Thompson. Their feedback—and reassurance—was exactly what I needed.

I don't know what I would do without my Slacker family: Mary, Jessica, Marisa, Susan, Ruby, Lyssa, Elvin, Rowyn, Meryl, Rosie, Jen, Alexis, Leslie, Nanci, and Jacki. Thank you for being an endless source of wisdom, tea, motivational GIFs, and controversial food opinions. I truly lucked out when I met all of you. Pitch Wars and Author Mentor Match—especially my mentors, M. K. England, Jamie Pacton, and Rebecca Schaeffer—helped me find my people, demystified the industry, and showed me what I was capable of; I owe a debt of gratitude to everyone who makes those programs possible year after year. And thank you to my fellow '22 debuts, an incredibly talented group of people I'm thrilled to have had a chance to get to know. I'm grateful for the conversations, the support, and everything I've learned from all of you.

Thank you to my family, especially my grandmothers, whose strength (and cooking) is a source of constant inspiration; my mom, who made sure I never ran out of books growing up, and my dad, who taught me to work hard and go after the things I wanted; and my sisters, whose humor and support has meant more to me than they probably realize.

And to you, readers, my final and most profound thanks. *The Prince of Nowhere* is yours now.